ANGELS IN BROOKLYN

An Ellis Angels Novel

Carole Lee Limata, RN, MSN

ISBN 10: 1-7974-7693-9
ISBN 13: 9781797476933

Dedication

**In memory of my mother,
Madeline Pampalone
1921 - 2018**

Novels by Carole Lee Limata

Ellis Angels:
The Nurses of Ellis Island Hospital

Ellis Angels on the Move:
Making a Difference in Brooklyn

Angels in Brooklyn:
An Ellis Angels Novel

Luna Babies

Table of Contents

Introduction

Nativity Settlement House and Health Clinic has opened once again to assist newly-arrived immigrants in 1926. Nurse Angie and Doctor Abe Goodwin, along with Nurse Adeline, continue their efforts to help immigrant families adapt to their new life in Brooklyn, New York.

Many come through the clinic's open doors: a single mother juggling two jobs to support her family, a young woman rushing to the clinic to save her infant and a widow struggling to care for her elderly mother and her young sons.

When a toddler is kidnapped in the neighborhood, the nurses band together and creatively unite to search for the child.

The immigrants are not the only ones facing daunting challenges. Nurse Adeline is confronted with a number of her own. She is forced to face her past when her dreams trigger long-forgotten memories of her military service, nursing wounded soldiers during World War One.

World War One Terminology *

Allied Powers: beginning in 1914 United Kingdom, British Empire, Australia, Canada, France, Russia, Japan, Greece, Siam, Hejas, Montenegro, Belgium, Italy, Portugal and Romania and in 1917 the United States

Blighty: originally slang for Great Britain; later used to indicate an injury that qualified a soldier to be transferred to Great Britain for recovery

Blue Pus: a wound that produces green or blue pus indicating a pseudo-monas bacterial infection

Carbolic: a disinfectant solution

Casualty Clearing Station (C.C.S.): the second stop on the *Casualty Evacuation Chain* usually located a mile from the front and equipped to treat hundreds of soldiers

Casualty Evacuation Chain: a series of medical stopovers through northern France leading to the French port of Calais

Central Powers: Germany, Austria-Hungry, Ottoman Empire and Bulgaria

Cholera Belt: a piece of flannel or knit fabric wrapped around the abdomen in the belief that this belt could prevent illnesses caused by cold weather

D-I: dangerously ill medical or surgical patients

Dressing Station: the first treatment and triage stop on the *Casualty Evacuation Chain* located steps away from the fighting front

Field Ambulance Convoy: a medical transport team carrying sick and wounded soldiers to a hospital

Gas Gangrene: a serious bacterial infection producing gas, edema, blistering and discoloring, often leading to necrosis and shock; patients with gas gangrene would be labeled *D-I* and isolated in private quarters

GSW: A gunshot wound

Huns, Jerries, Kraut, Fritz and Company: derogatory names for soldiers in the German army

Luftwaffe: German Air Force

Mackintosh: a raincoat made from rubberized material

M.O.: a medical officer, a physician

Quartermaster: an army officer in charge of the distribution of supplies

R.A.M.C.: Great Britain's Royal Army Medical Corps

S-I: seriously ill medical or surgical patients

Sister Suzy Bag: a sack used to hold a soldier's possessions; women on the home front in Great Britain sewed shirts, bags and pajamas for the soldiers

Stationary Tent Hospital: unlike a mobile medical unit, this type of tented hospital was designed to stay in one place.

Tommies: soldiers in the British army

Trench Fever: a serious bacterial infection lasting less than a week and characterized by a headache, rash and fever; believed to be caused by lice infestation

Trench Foot: a condition caused by living in the wet trenches and continually being exposed to a damp and dirty environment

Trench Foot Buddy: during WW I, a partnering system was implemented to decrease the number of trench foot cases; soldiers were paired and assigned to check the feet of their partner daily

Trephine: an instrument used in a surgical procedure to cut a round opening to extract bone or relieve pressure

Triage: a system of evaluating the severity of injuries among a large group in order to treat the most severely injured first

VAD: a nickname for Voluntary Aid Detachment, English women who volunteered during the war to care for sick and injured soldiers but were not professionally trained nurses

*World War One terminology is written in italics to assist the reader.

Chapter One

～

January 1918
Stationary Hospital #16
Le Treport, France

Their helping hands make spirits soar
As angels soothe the wounds of war.

The rain began at midnight, pounding the sides of the hospital tent and soaking through to the inside of the canvas. The nurse listened and waited, hoping for a break in the weather before she began her rounds to check the soldiers under her care. When she couldn't wait any longer, she armed herself with her *mackintosh*, boots and gloves. Reaching for her lantern, she trudged out into the dark of night and braced herself for the unexpected since anything could happen on a night like this. Only a week earlier a strong gale had downed an entire ward tent, awakening everyone in camp and hastening a mad rush to rescue the soldiers sleeping inside.

Shards of icy rain pelted her slicker as she carefully balanced on the mud-soaked floor boards set down between the tents. With only a flicker of light from her lantern, she cautiously made her way to Ward Tent B9. As she approached the tent, a great gust of wet wind whipped opened the entrance flap. Once inside, it took all her strength to secure the flap by lacing it closed. She hooked an army-issue wool blanket over the opening to create an additional barrier from the strong wind.

Echoes of deep nasal snores and heavy breathing filled the musty air ahead of her. She looked over at the young Aussie sleeping closest to the entrance of the tent. Although he bore the brunt of the rain, he slept soundly in his waterlogged bed.

Poor lad, bless him, these boys can sleep through anything, even this frigid cold.

The fire in the center of the tent was in danger of going out. The nurse stirred the embers and stacked four cords of wood in a log-cabin fashion, trying not to smother the last remaining coals. Removing her wool gloves, she set them down close to the fire to dry. Her chilblained fingers felt numb from the cold. She briskly rubbed her hands together before attending to the sixteen soldiers in the surgical ward. After rounds, changing the bed linens of the slumbering Australian would be her first priority.

They called the boy *Lucky*. Almost everyone in camp had a nickname designated to him because of something he did or some unique physical characteristic. For example, the orderly who sang through his chores was given the name *Caruso*. The tiny mess cook who didn't quite reach a height of five feet was simply called *Shorty*. Sergeant Kingsley was labeled *The King* by some. The boy called *Lucky* had named himself. After the *M.O.*, the medical officer, announced that the boy's right leg would be saved from amputation, the boy shouted: "Just call me *Lucky*!" From that time on, everyone in camp did just that.

The nurse looked down upon the sleeping soldier and nudged him gently. His chunky cheeks and sleepy eyes revealed that he was a youth of no more than fifteen years of age.

"Do you think I'll be leaving for *Blighty* first thing in the morning, Sister?" he asked her.

"Perhaps," she whispered, "after the doctor makes a final check of your leg wound. Of course, that's if the *jerries* don't mess with the tracks again."

Twice that month, the *Luftwaffe* had blown up the train tracks leading to the port of Calais where the ferries sailed for Dover. A railroad delay not only detained the next convoy of injured soldiers, it interfered with the daily shipment of food and supplies that the field hospitals received from Great Britain.

"They gave me my tickets two days ago."

"Yes, I know," she answered, looking up at the two green tickets taped to the wall near his bed. The green color indicated that he would travel as a surgical patient. One ticket would be tied to his pajamas during his trip to Dover. The other was his return ticket to Calais to be used after his recuperation in a London hospital. The *M.O.*s were often in the habit of awarding the *Blighty* tickets early on as an incentive for healing.

After the nurse took the soldier's temperature and helped him out of his soggy nightclothes, she made preparations to change his leg dressing. Before she pulled off his bloody bandage, she placed a small lavender pillow near his head. Puffy pouches of dried lavender were regularly found among the Red Cross supplies shipped from England. They had been tenderly hand sewn and carefully packaged by the Women's Volunteer Auxiliary of St. Andrew's Church in Shepardswell.

Such thoughtful ladies, I wonder if they know how much their lavender pillows are needed to mask the stench of infection.

Satisfied that her patient was clean and dry, the nurse advanced to the next soldier. When she completed her checks of the boys in

Surgical Tent Ward B9, she geared up to move on to Surgical Tent Ward B10. She repeated this pattern of ward checks through the night as she traveled from tent to tent: dressing up for the harsh weather, searching for each tent in pitch darkness, unburdening herself of her cumbersome outer garments upon her arrival and bundling up once again after her ward checks were completed. Although there was a certain repetitive element in her night duty routine, there was nothing ordinary or monotonous about her service in the military hospital. In the wee hours of the morning, she fought an ever-pressing desire to sleep in order to remain hypervigilant and alert. She knew that observing the slightest deviation from the norm meant the difference between a patient's recovery and his decline. A lost life was a high price to pay for a distraction.

Occasionally she allowed herself to rest at a tiny makeshift table close to the fire in the middle of each tent, taking the necessary time to document her nursing care. Moments before the break of dawn, she noticed the staccato sounds of the rain had stopped. It amused her that the rain would cease as her night duty was ending.

An hour later, she gave her morning report to the day-shift nurse and welcomed the rush of morning air that blasted her when she opened the tent door-flap. To her delight, she found the hospital camp covered in an inch of snow. The light sprinkling of white powder covered up the blood stains on the weathered planks of wood that lay buried beneath the snow, concealing all evidence of war.

The campsite was arranged in two straight lines with twelve large round tents in each row. The medical patients were placed in A Line and the surgical patients were assigned to B Line. However, when large convoys of sick and injured soldiers arrived, medical and surgical

units often overlapped. The northside tents housed the quarters of the
M.O.s, the medical officers, and the Royal Army Medical Corps orderlies, the R.A.M.C.s. The nurses and VADs camped in south camp,
while the mess hall and the pastor's service tent were conveniently
situated in the center of camp. The *quartermaster's* supply tent and the
laundry tent were located to the far left of camp, close to the railroad
tracks and the white cliffs overlooking the channel.

The nurse looked down at her muddied winter boots. Her stained
apron, which had been starched and pristine the evening before, was
now splattered with blood, soot and ashes. It always amazed her how
efficiently the local French women worked their magic on her stained
uniforms using only *carbolic* soap and bleach. Although she knew no
one was working in the laundry tent at such an early hour, she decided
to exchange her soiled apron and white arm-covers for a freshly
starched set before heading to the mess tent for breakfast.

Her boots made bulky impressions in the soft snow as she walked
toward the laundry tent. She heard the sound of the German biplanes
and a faraway blast before seeing the two night bombers in the morning sky. Because the base camp sirens remained silent, she continued
on fearlessly, aware of the Geneva Treaty which protected military
hospitals from enemy attack. Despite this, she looked up to notice a
strange silent flare in the sky just before the laundry tent exploded in
a flash twenty feet ahead of her.

As the bomb landed, the young nurse was shoved to the ground.
Dazed, it took her a moment to realize that the heavy weight pin-
ning her down was a sharp-eyed sentry who had witnessed the attack.
The nurse attempted to speak, to tell him she couldn't breathe, but
the words would not come out. The last sound she heard before she

fainted was the base camp emergency siren. A minute later, the soldier slowly lifted himself off the nurse. Her body lay limp beneath him. The soldier attempted to revive her by shaking her.

"Miss Adeline, Adeline, Adeline, are you okay?"

Chapter Two

❧

January 1926
The Waldorf Astoria Hotel
The Steingold Suite
New York City

Like a hurricane, fast and furious, it came without warning,
Quietly unleashing its terror in the early hours of morning.

"Adeline, Adeline, Adeline, are you okay?"

"Humm…what?"

"Adeline, dear, wake up! You were trying to tell me that you couldn't breathe."

"Oh, Harry, what did I say?"

"You said you couldn't breathe. Were you dreaming?"

"Yes, I was dreaming," Adeline mumbled. "I'm sorry I woke you. I was in France again."

"Do you want to talk about it?"

"The war…it was the war."

"The great one?"

"Yes."

"I know you served in France for nearly two years, but I don't remember you having these dreams until recently."

"I thought I had made peace with my wartime service, but this summer I began to dream of the war again. It was about a month after we adopted baby Henry."

"Why would our baby trigger dreams of war?"

"I think it's because of the boys."

"Which boys?"

"The young soldiers, the *tommies*, they were only teenagers. Some never lived to see their eighteenth birthday. They lied about their age when they enlisted."

"Yes, you told me. They had a military age and a real age."

"They were just kids. I can still see their chubby cheeks on their innocent round faces, even the teen acne they developed living in the trenches. Perhaps I've been dreaming of them because I'm a mother now. The thought of Henry going off to war horrifies me. He could easily become one of them. Some of the lads were only fifteen years old."

"Yes, I see, a mother's worry."

"It's every mother's worry, I suppose. There's nothing any of us can do about it."

"Would it help to talk to someone, a doctor perhaps?"

"I don't know, Harry. If my dreams are about a mother's worry, is there really anything anyone can do?"

"You were frightened. You called out that you couldn't breathe. Do you remember that?" Harry asked.

"I remember that I wasn't frightened in the dream. It was early morning and I was walking in a fresh powder of snow that had recently fallen. Without warning, I watched as the *jerries* bombed one of our base tents. I was saved by a soldier who jumped on top of me and crushed me in order to protect me. I wasn't afraid. You see, I knew I was dreaming because the Germans would never undertake a bombing mission in inclement weather. The *Luftwaffe* always waited for the clearest, brightest night sky. The night bombers were often instructed to abort their mission if the weather changed suddenly."

"You told me they weren't supposed to attack hospitals."

"Our camp was so close to the railroad tracks that they used the excuse that their mark was the tracks."

"You said you couldn't breathe? How do you feel now?"

"Fine, Harry. I'm perfectly fine. It was just a dream. I was dreaming about a soldier who protected me by covering me with his body. I remember being knocked down by the weight of him."

"I'm glad he saved you. He's a man after my own heart. I would have done the same...jumped on top of you to protect you in a split second."

"Really?"

"Really, I love you, Adeline, more than I can ever say. I have always loved you from the moment I first met you. When I think that I actually let you go off and sign up for the war in France, I hate myself. You could have been killed."

"Most of the time, I felt safe. I wasn't stationed near the front.

"I don't even want to think about you living in a tent in the freezing weather."

"It wasn't always winter. I remember delightful days in the spring and summer. In the spring, we would roll up the sides of the tents and they would become open-air hospitals. My friend Mary would drag me through field and forest in search of wild orchids, violets and anemones to spruce up the wards. There were days when the wards were filled with garlands of wildflowers and music from the gramophones." Adeline smiled. "We played the same songs over and over again because we only had a handful of discs. In the summer, we would go down to the beach."

"When was there time for that?"

"Between convoys, after the boys left, we cleaned the tents and waited for a new convoy to arrive. Sometimes there was a day or two between convoys when we were allowed to walk to the village or relax on the beach."

"What if a convoy arrived and you weren't there?"

"The all-hands-bugle would call us and we would all run back to camp."

"To start the process over again," Harry said as he embraced Adeline. "I thank the Lord that it's over and you're safe."

"Me, too, Harry, me, too."

"Maybe it would help if you talked to Doctor Abe about these dreams."

"Oh, he's far too busy right now with the reopening celebration at the settlement house. I don't want to bother him."

"Have you talked to Angie?"

"No, only to you...right now."

"Well, I'm glad you did, but promise me you'll talk to Abe or Angie."

"I promise, Harry, but not tomorrow. Tomorrow is their big day. It's the reception for the blessing of the children's daycare center."

"I know. My mother has been baking all week for the event."

"The bishop and the alderman are coming. A reporter from *The Brooklyn Bugle* is expected."

"Well then," Harry whispered, as he cradled his wife in his arms and covered her with the blanket. "Let's try to get some sleep."

"Okay. Night, Harry."

"Good night, Darling."

Chapter Three

❧

January 1926
Nativity Settlement House
Williamsburg, Brooklyn

Neighbors come to eat and play to
A party planned for opening day.

As Adeline and Harry Steingold slept in their bedroom suite at the Waldorf Astoria Hotel in Manhattan, eight miles away across the East River the section of Brooklyn called *Williamsburg* slowly awakened. Mr. Theodor, the neighborhood milkman, was finishing the last of his milk deliveries on his daily route. He nodded a *good morning* to Mike, the iceman, who was hitching up his horse wagon, preparing to begin his morning rounds. The intoxicating aroma of freshly baked bread floated across Graham Avenue from Milano's Bakery, where the baker's wife, Loretta Milano, was placing a dozen freshly-baked stuffoli pastries in the bakery shop window. Next door at Penzolli's Pork Shop, the butcher's son was sprinkling an extra layer of sawdust on the hardwood floors. After Mario, the grocer, pried open the fruit and vegetable crates he purchased the night before, he selected the freshest samples to display outside on his fruit stand. Further up the street at the Jewish delicatessen, Jakub Werner was making the potato knishes that he would sell later in the day while his wife Dinah was preparing a fresh batch of potato salad.

Around the corner at the Nativity Settlement House and Health Clinic on Johnson Avenue, newlywed Angie Goodwin sat at the table in the kitchen utility room reviewing the to-do list she had prepared the week before. The list had been endless when she began but by tackling a little each day, Angie managed to accomplish everything that needed to be done in preparation for the open house festivities scheduled to begin that morning. Dressed in her starched white uniform, nurse's cap and white shoes, Angie looked every bit the poised and professional nurse she was. On the inside, however, she was nervous and excited for the day to begin. For reassurance, she decided to make a final inspection of the grounds before the guests arrived.

The front room of Nativity House was a large reception room with a central fireplace. The hardwood floors had been waxed and polished in preparation for the day. Extra folding tables had been borrowed from Nativity Church and were arranged in a horseshoe pattern in the middle of the room, ready to receive the cookies and pastries that Mrs. Steingold and Mama Myers would be bringing. Both women had spent the better part of the week baking treats and delicacies for the big event.

Angie opened the double doors leading into the cheerful examination area. Two large rooms were divided into six private exam stations by colorful cotton curtains hanging from the ceiling. Each station's chrome cabinets gleamed and its glass shelves sparkled. The linoleum floors were spotless and all potentially harmful equipment was locked away. Her husband's lab coat hung on the back door, freshly starched and ironed, ready to wear.

From the examination area, Angie walked directly into another large room similar in size to the front room. Painted in pastel pinks and blues, the room had a large rainbow hand-painted on the rear wall. Formerly used for childcare, this area was now reserved for classes and community meetings. The backdoor led into the rear courtyard where a two-story building and play structure had recently been built, replacing the shabby horse stable which once stood there. The new afterschool center would provide social activities and tutoring for the children in the neighborhood. Although financed with grant money from the Steingold Foundation, it was designed and constructed by a group of able volunteers from the neighborhood.

It was at the entrance of the afterschool center that she found her husband Abe, tacking a bright red ribbon to each end of the doorway of the new building.

"Oh, Angie, you're just in time. How does this look? Is the ribbon straight?"

"It's perfect, Abe. Where did you find such a large ribbon?"

"I walked down to DeSouza's Florist last night and asked him if he had any extra ribbon to spare."

"Is that what you were up to?"

"Yes, I wanted to surprise you. After the bishop gives his blessing, we will ask him to cut the ribbon. Then the center will officially open. Now, all we need is a pair of scissors."

"I have my bandage scissors right here in my pocket," Angie said as she tapped her uniform pocket. "When it's time, I'll hand them to the bishop."

"After that, we will begin the tours."

"Perfect. I think everything is in order and ready for today except…"

"Except what?"

"Except you, dear."

"What do you mean?" Abe looked puzzled.

"You look a sight! What have you been up to?"

"I was painting the trim inside. There were some spots we missed."

"Well, you have white paint in your hair. Hurry and wash up. Your mother and brother will be here in an hour."

"I guess I lost track of time. Is it that late already? I'll go upstairs right now."

"Your lab coat is pressed and ready. I brought it down. It's in the exam room."

"Thanks, Angie, now I need only one more thing."

"What's that, doctor?"

"A kiss from my bride…"

"Oh, Abe!" Angie smiled as she put her arms around her husband and kissed him.

"Thank you, my dear. That's all the incentive I need."

"There now, off you go."

"I promise I won't be long," Abe called out as he hurried upstairs to their second floor apartment.

The first to arrive at Nativity House that morning was Abe's mother, Mama Myers. She was carrying a basket of Italian pignola cookies. Her son, Sam, followed, carrying three boxes of biscotti and pizzelles.

"Good Morning, Angie, I think Mama baked enough cookies to feed everyone in the entire borough of Brooklyn," Sam announced.

"It certainly looks that way, Sam."

"Now, now, you can never have enough. All the people will be looking for something to eat," Mama Myers insisted.

"But remember, Mrs. Steingold is also bringing…"

Angie was interrupted by a knock on the door.

"Help!"

Sam put his bundle down and quickly opened the front door to find his fiancée balancing another three boxes of cookies.

"Let me help you, Maureen," Sam said, reaching for the top box which was about to fall. "I was coming out to the car to carry these in for you."

Maureen laughed. "I thought I could carry everything in by myself."

"Let me help, too," Angie said as she reached for another box of cookies. "How are you this morning?"

"Fine, Angie, but I was so excited about today that I could hardly sleep last night."

"Me, too," Angie agreed, giving Maureen a big kiss on her cheek.

Maureen put a box of cookies on the kitchen table. "My mother baked this box of shortbread cookies for us. Do you think we'll have enough for everyone, Angie?"

Angie smiled. "Oh yes, look at all this. Harry's mother has been baking also. She'll be here any minute. She's bringing rugelach and macaroons."

"Mama said the rugelach won't be as popular as her biscotti," Sam teased.

"Stop, Sam. I did not say that," Mama Myers scolded.

"Angie, we now have cookie samples from all over the world."

"We do and our assortment of cookies reflects the diversity of the neighborhood, doesn't it?"

At that moment, the doorbell rang three times. When Angie opened the front door, five-year-old Sadie Steingold still had her hand on the doorbell. "I finally reached the doorbell, Aunt Angie. I stretched up as far as I could."

"Yes, Sadie, I can see that. Good for you. Oh my, Sadie, you look beautiful today."

"Grandma Steingold bought me a new dress," Sadie announced proudly as she turned around to model her pink dress revealing a big satin bow in the back. The dress was made of a delicate soft corduroy fabric which perfectly matched her shoes.

"Sadie, you only have to ring a doorbell once, dear. Ring it once and wait for the people to come along," Adeline told Sadie as she walked into the room with her husband, Harry. Adeline greeted Angie with a kiss on her cheek. "I'm sorry for the noise, Angie."

"No problem at all. How is everyone today?"

"I couldn't sleep," Adeline said.

"I couldn't sleep either," Maureen chimed in. "I was too excited."

All eyes turned to ten-month-old baby Henry who was in his father's arms.

"…And who is this handsome young fellow who has grown so much since the last time I saw him?" Maureen asked. "Oh, Harry, Henry's getting so big. Can I hold him?"

"Sure, here you go, but I'm warning you, he's getting heavy." When Harry handed the baby to Maureen, Henry immediately started to cry and reached his hands out toward Adeline.

"He certainly knows who his mommy is, doesn't he?" Maureen said as she bounced the baby in her arms.

"Yes, in the short time since we adopted him, he's gotten very attached to us. He especially loves his big sister, Sadie."

"Angie, I think we should keep the front door open, after all..."

"It is an open house!" Angie quickly finished Maureen's sentence. "I'll put the doorstop in." When Angie opened the front door, Leonora and her parents arrived.

"Hello, everyone!" Leonora announced. "My parents came with me today. Angie, Adeline, I would like to introduce my parents, Mr. and Mrs. Bartoli."

"Buon Giorno! Welcome! We are so happy to finally meet you," Angie said, shaking Mr. Bartoli's hand.

"We baked some cookies for you," Mrs. Bartoli said as she offered Angie a box of cookies.

"Thank you so much. You didn't have to bring anything, but we will certainly put them to good use. I'm sure they're delicious. Mrs. Bartoli, we've been so impressed with your daughter since she's been working with us at the settlement house. You should be proud of her," Angie said.

Mr. Bartoli answered, "Yes, she wants-a to work and help others. She's a modern day woman."

"Indeed she is," Angie agreed. "Come, Leonora, introduce your parents to the others."

"Papa, Mama, this is Maureen O'Shaughnessy. She's our visiting nurse in Williamsburg and this is her fiancé, Sam Goodwin."

"Nice-a to meet you. Are you-a Doctor Goodwin?"

"No," Sam laughed. "I'm the undertaker in the family. My brother, Abraham, is the doctor."

"Well," said Mrs. Bartoli with a smile, "it's good to have one of each in the family, isn't it?"

The bishop arrived next. After him, their alderman appeared. A reporter from *The Brooklyn Bugle* came with his photographer, Jim. Soon after, the neighbors in the community trickled in and gathered around the refreshment table until the reception room was filled with people.

When it was time for the ceremonies to begin, Dr. Abe Goodwin made the opening remarks and welcomed everyone. After the bishop's invocation, Angie fingered the bandage scissors in her uniform pocket, preparing to hand them to the bishop.

"Wait!" *The Brooklyn Bugle* reporter asked, "Can we take a few photos first?"

"Yes!" Abe agreed. The first picture was of Angie and Abe standing with the bishop, posing to appear as if they were about to cut the red ribbon.

Angie called for Maureen and Leonora. "Please take one with our visiting nurse, Maureen, and Nativity House's very first volunteer, Leonora. The new center is their special project."

"Of course," Jim, the photographer said.

After the second photograph, Jim asked, "Now, may I take a photograph of the Steingold family and the bishop?"

At the photographer's request, Adeline and Harry stepped forward and posed with the bishop.

"Let's bring the children in," he suggested.

After *The Brooklyn Bugle* photographer took the picture of the Steingold family with Sadie and Henry, the red ribbon was cut and the festivities began.

Chapter Four

The Following Day
The Waldorf Astoria Hotel
The Steingold Suite
New York City

The picture of her family,
Will someday solve a mystery.

As Harry Steingold prepared to leave for work from the Steingold Suite at the Waldorf Astoria Hotel, Philip, the bellboy assigned to the hotel's penthouse apartments, emerged from the elevator with an armload of morning newspapers.

"Good Morning, Mr. Steingold and Mrs. Steingold! Special delivery for you, here are all your morning newspapers, hot off the presses."

"Ah, the papers, you're just in time, Phil," Harry said. "What's the weather like out there today?"

"Cold but clear and sunny."

Adeline reached for the newspapers that Philip was carrying. "Good Morning, Philip, let me take those from you."

"Thank you, Mrs. Steingold."

"Adeline, I'd like to read the New York paper in the car, but keep the rest here and I'll read them tonight."

"Okay, I'm going to look through *The Brooklyn Bugle*. Have a wonderful day, dear."

Adeline watched as her husband walked down the hall, turned and waved goodbye. As he entered the elevator, she blew him a kiss. Once inside the hotel suite, she prepared a cup of coffee in the kitchen and brought it out into the living room. After she found a comfortable spot on the luxurious mohair sofa, she eagerly opened *The Brooklyn Bugle*.

To her surprise, the entire front page of *The Brooklyn Bugle* was covered with the picture of her family with the bishop as he pretended to cut the red ribbon at the Nativity House celebration. There was Adeline, looking radiantly happy, standing next to her handsome husband who carried baby Henry in his arms. Sadie held onto Adeline with one hand and with the other waved to the cameraman. The photographer had captured the happy smiles of both baby Henry and Sadie as they looked directly into the camera.

The headlines read: *Steingolds Finance Settlement House in Brooklyn.*

Adeline was shocked that *The Brooklyn Bugle* reporter had chosen to feature her family as the cover story, rather than focusing on Angie and Abe who were the founders of Nativity House.

Adeline jumped up from the sofa and quickly sprang into action.

She called for Rachel, the children's nurse. "I'm going to take Sadie to school earlier than usual today. Please help me wake her and get her ready for school."

"Yes, Mrs. Steingold. Shall I wake up Master Henry also?" Rachel asked.

"I should like him to stay with you while I drive Sadie to school. No need to wake him."

Thirty minutes later, Adeline and Sadie were in the family's Studebaker, driving over the Williamsburg Bridge. Adeline parked in front of Nativity Catholic School. After walking Sadie to her kindergarten class, she hurried back to the car and drove around the block to the settlement house. She parked and jumped out of the car.

The morning edition of *The Brooklyn Bugle* had already been delivered and was lying in the hallway. She picked it up and opened the front door. The aroma of freshly brewed coffee filled the reception room. Adeline followed it into the kitchen where she found Dr. Abe enjoying a cup of morning coffee.

Abe greeted her with a smile and a kiss on the cheek. "Good Morning, Adeline. You're here early this morning."

"I came as soon as I saw it."

"What did you see?" Abe asked.

"This!" Adeline said as she opened the newspaper and showed Abe the front page.

"Let me see. What a great picture, Adeline. The four of you certainly make a beautiful family."

"That's not the point."

"What's the point?" Abe asked.

"Read the headlines."

"I did."

"Abe, a picture of you and Angie should have been on the *Bugle's* front page this morning. Why would the reporter put the Steingold family on the cover?"

"The Steingolds are news. Everyone in town has seen or shopped at Steingold Jewelers. The newspaper editor knows that people are interested in reading about the family behind the famous name."

"...But you and Angie created Nativity House."

"Yes, but Angie and I are ordinary people. We're not the celebrities. You are."

"Well, I don't agree but I am relieved you're not offended."

Angie came into the kitchen and asked, "Now, what's all this arguing about? Hi, Adeline, you're here early this morning."

"Yes, I came as soon as I saw the front page of *The Bugle*. Angie, look at this morning's paper. I feel terrible. It should have been you and Abe on the front page."

"Let me see." When Adeline handed Angie the newspaper, Angie smiled. "Oh, Ade, this is a lovely photograph of you and the children. They are adorable. You should request a copy and frame it."

"Angie, it should be you and Abe on the front page."

"No, I don't think so but I hope the article mentions all the work that Leonora and Maureen did to get the children's center off the ground."

"You're really not offended?"

"No, Adeline. It was Harry who saved the settlement house. We would have had to close it down when our funding ran out a few months ago. The bootleggers were financing the settlement house as a front for their operation. After we learned that, it was your husband who proposed a new fiscal plan to the bishop."

"Yes, but Abe should have been featured. It was his dream from the start."

"Listen, Adeline, the important thing is that the settlement house has once again opened its doors. We are bigger and better than ever." Abe added, "...and this extra publicity won't hurt us. It will help us."

Angie agreed. "We are indebted to Harry and his foundation for all they've done to support the settlement house. I hope Harry knows how much we appreciate his efforts."

"Yes, of course, he does, Angie."

"Good, then he deserves to be recognized, doesn't he?"

"I suppose so," Adeline smiled. "He has been wonderful."

"Yes, we've been blessed by his generosity and yours, too. Both of you opened your hearts to us, and look what you have done for Sadie and Harry when you adopted them."

"Thank you, Angie."

"Now enough of this discussion," Abe said, filling up three coffee cups. "May I interest you ladies in a freshly-brewed cup of coffee and some biscotti? I found a whole box of biscotti hidden away in the coffee cupboard this morning."

"Your mother hid them there yesterday. She was determined to save an extra box for us."

"Just a half cup, please," Adeline said. "I have a new mothers' class starting at nine."

Angie looked at the kitchen clock on the wall, "...and the clinic should be opening soon."

"Let's enjoy our coffee, ladies, and then off we'll go to start the first day at our new and improved Nativity House!"

Later that evening, as Adeline was sitting on her vanity bench brushing her hair, Harry entered the bedroom. "Are you still feeling blue about our picture in the paper, Adeline?"

"Yes, it bothers me."

"I know you're upset but remember today's news is tomorrow's trash. Everyone will have forgotten the photograph by morning."

"But..."

"Isn't there anything I can do to cheer you up?" Harry asked.

"No, what's done is done. I don't believe anyone can do anything."

"Well, there may be something. I've been thinking. I can call the editor and ask him to consider writing an article on Abe and Angie."

"Really?"

"Yes, it would be additional publicity for the center and make an interesting read."

"I agree. Perhaps you can suggest that he wait a little while so that Angie and Abe think it's the editor's idea."

"I'll suggest doing it in a month or two, not right away. Now, do you feel a little better?"

"Much better, Harry, it's a wonderful idea. Thank you."

"…And thank you, my dear."

"For what?"

"For being my wife," Harry whispered as he bent to kiss Adeline *goodnight*. Offering her his hand, he led her into bed. "Now, I suggest we both try to get a good night's sleep tonight."

"Good night, Harry."

"Sweet dreams, Adeline."

Chapter Five

∾

February 1918
Stationary Hospital #16
Le Treport, France

With the dawn comes bitter frost,
Frozen pipes and their water's lost.

Long before sunrise, the bitter cold awakened the nurse from her slumber. Determined to get a good night's sleep, she had prepared her bed the night before in anticipation of a frosty morning. She slept with three pairs of socks and a knit cap which she pulled down to cover her ears. Over her flannel nightgown, she wore the two cashmere sweaters that her mother had carefully packaged and sent to her from home. After she arranged her bunk with three layers of army-issue, khaki-colored, wool blankets, she buried a piping hot water bottle beneath them. Lastly, when she was securely positioned inside her cozy cocoon, she covered herself with her tapestry traveling rug for extra warmth.

Fatigue aided her sleep. She remained asleep until her frosty fingers and icy nose awakened her. Attempting to steal a few extra minutes of sleep, she tucked her face under the blankets.

Margaux, the village girl who filled the nurses' washbasins with fresh water every morning, was the first one to enter the tent. Wearing a brown rabbit-skin cape, she knocked on the floorboard to alert the nurse of her presence.

"Je suis de'sole'e. Sorry to wake you, Madame. There's no water this morning. Le Commandant says the main water pipe froze and broke during the night. It may take hours before its fixed. All I can do for you this morning is to stir up the embers to warm your tent."

Adeline lingered under her bedroll until she felt the warmth of the fire. She remembered the *field ambulance convoy* that had come in the night before. The soldiers arrived covered in a dusting of lime-colored earth that they had picked up along the route. The nurses and *VAD*s did their best to cut through the muddy, blood-crusted uniforms of the soldiers in order to give them bed baths. There were a large number of *GSW*s, gun-shot wounds, and embedded shrapnel cases. When the nurses *triaged* the boys, they isolated two *D-I*s, dangerously-ill cases, two soldiers with *gas gangrene* fever.

It had taken quite some time for the soldiers to settle down for the night. They used a variety of names to address the nurses when they called for assistance: sister, miss, misses, madame, mame, mother and nurse.

"Sister, is there anything you can do for my shivers?"

"Miss, can you get me another pillow?"

"Do you have an extra blanket, Misses?"

"Please move my arm over a bit, Madame? It's throbbing in this position."

"Mame, do you think they will operate in the morning?"

"Mother, will I lose my leg?"

"Water, please, Nurse, my throat is so dry."

With so many needing care and attention, Adeline anticipated a busy morning. The day's scheduled *trephine* surgeries would have to be postponed until there was enough water to wash and sterilize the equipment. The boys needed more cleaning and the *trench foot* cases required repeated washings. She tried not to think about the complaints she would hear when she announced that morning coffee would not be served. Their breakfast would consist of hard cheese and stale crackers.

When Adeline felt the cold rubber buried at the bottom of her bedroll, it gave her an idea. If the nurses collected all the hot-water bottles they had distributed the night before, there might be enough water left to boil for dressing changes.

As Adeline wriggled out of her bedding, she grabbed the hot-water bottle. She carefully measured and poured out one-half of a cup of water into her washbasin. That was all she needed to wet a washrag to wash her face. She had enough water left over to brush her teeth. Fighting with the metal tube of toothpaste proved to be a useless endeavor. As hard she tired, the frozen toothpaste in the tube remained stiff and solid and would not budge from its casing.

Adeline had become remarkably adept at dressing efficiently and quickly that winter. She learned that the secret was in placing everything she needed on the wooden box next to her bed the night before. This included her wool leggings, a *cholera belt* for under her uniform and two sweater vests for over it. After she tugged on her boots, she hiked up her uniform skirt by tucking the center of it into her waist belt. These improvised trousers would get her to the ward tents without the skirt of her uniform billowing in the wind.

She entered Ward Tent A1 to find most of the soldiers sleeping. After the night-duty nurse hurriedly gave her report and left, Adeline decided to use the few quiet minutes to prepare her medication orders.

She wanted to be ready to distribute the morning medications as soon as the boys woke up.

When she found six broken medicine bottles, her first thought was that an animal had found his way into the pharmacy cupboard. Then she remembered that an English nurse had once cautioned her that some of the pharmaceuticals and lotions occasionally froze solid in the wintertime. It had been so cold during the night that some of the medicines and syrups had turned to ice and expanded, breaking their glass containers. She also noticed that the beaker of glass thermometers had transformed into a rather odd-looking glass sculpture when the carbolic bath they were soaking in had frozen into ice.

After lining up the unbroken bottles of ferrous citrate, cod liver and castor oil near the fire to melt, Adeline sat down to write a nursing note on what had occurred that morning. To her surprise, she discovered that her fountain pen would not release its ink.

Nurse Mary opened the tent entrance flap and called out to her. Mary was dressed for a summer day, wearing only her uniform and no outer gear.

"Come, Adeline. Follow me. I found crocuses in the meadow, popping out through the snow. Come. We must pick them for the nurses."

Adeline put down her fountain pen and ran after Mary for fear that her friend would catch cold. Mary was already at the hilltop cemetery adjacent to the Hospital for Caregivers when Adeline reached her. She followed her into the cemetery. Mary called out to her. "Adeline, there are too many tombstones. I don't have enough flowers for all the nurses' graves. Why, there seem to be hundreds. I need to pick more cowslip for all of the nurses buried here. Will you help me?"

"No, Mary, you aren't going anywhere. You must return to camp with me. You will catch your death dressed like that."

"No matter, Adeline, I have already died," Mary called out as she disappeared into a gravesite.

Suddenly remembering that she had abandoned her post and left her patients unattended, Adeline hurried back to base camp. Entering the hospital tent, she discovered that every cot on the ward had turned into an infant's crib. Each crib held a little boy, crying with his hands outstretched, reaching out for his mother.

Chapter Six

ॐ

January 1926
The Waldorf Astoria Hotel
The Steingold Suite
New York City

All too soon, the good die young
To leave the world with songs unsung.

Adeline sat up in bed. "Was that the baby crying?"

Suddenly awakened, Harry mumbled, "I didn't hear anything."

"Harry, I thought I heard baby Henry crying."

"Listen. I don't hear a sound, maybe you were dreaming."

"I suppose I was."

"Another war dream, was it?"

"I'm afraid so, Harry."

Adeline got out of bed and put on her robe. "I want to be certain. I'm going to check the baby. I'll be right back."

Adeline found her ten-month-old baby in his crib, sleeping peacefully on his tummy with his bottom up in the air. She leaned over the crib railing to listen to his breathing. When she kissed the back of his head, she caught a whiff of his sweaty hair. She loved the smell of the baby and stood up on her tiptoes to savor his sweet scent.

Satisfied that her son was sleeping safely, she returned to the bedroom to find her husband had turned on the bedside table lamp. She sat down on the bedroom chaise. "Have you ever noticed how good he smells when he sleeps?"

Harry didn't hesitate to answer, "...like fresh bread right out of the oven."

"...and his toes."

"Yes, after you take his little white shoes and socks off."

"He knows we smell his feet."

"How do you know that?" Harry asked.

"The other day, I took off his socks, and he put his toes right up to my nose and laughed."

"Adeline, was Henry upset and crying in your dream?"

"No, the soldiers had turned into babies and they all were crying. I had abandoned my post to follow Mary. When I returned to the ward, I found them all crying for their mothers."

"What happened to Mary?"

"In my dream or in life?" Adeline asked.

Harry got out of bed and cuddled up close to his wife on the huge chaise lounge. "Tell me both, Adeline."

"Well, in my dream, Mary was picking flowers in the meadow. She said she needed the flowers to place on the graves of the nurses who had died and were buried in the cemetery near Dieppe. Hundreds had died during the war."

"There was an influenza epidemic in 1918."

"Yes, over two hundred died that year, but there were more who died before that."

"Innocent victims of the war..."

"The nurses only wanted to make things better for the boys, especially Mary. She was my bunkmate, the kindest kid ever. With her blue eyes, blonde hair and bright smile, she was all sunshine and light. We had worked together at Ellis Island Hospital before the war, you know."

"No, I didn't know."

"She would bring hair ribbons and candy to the children on the wards when she came back from her day off in the city. She was always hugging and kissing the children. After that, Sister Hanover mandated that the nurses were not allowed to kiss the children."

"Does she still work at Ellis?"

"No."

"What happened to her?"

"She died in France. One morning, after working a night shift, I returned to our tent to find that it had sprung a leak during the night. It was raining directly down on Mary's cot. Mary was sound asleep. That kid could sleep through anything. During the night, rather than move from her bed, Mary plopped her *mackintosh* over her and slept under it. When I touched Mary to wake her, she was burning with fever. I somehow managed to dress her and walk her over to the medical officers' tent. She was immediately transferred to the Hospital for Caregivers up on the hill…

"I stayed with her throughout the day, giving her frequent alcohol baths to lower her temperature. She was struggling to breathe. The nurses gave her a small dose of morphine to help open her airway and ease her labored breathing. I left her when her respirations relaxed and slowed down and I reported for night duty. In the morning, I returned to the hospital. When I arrived, I discovered that Mary's bed was empty. I was certain that she had been transferred. I went from ward to ward searching for her. Finally, I inquired."

"What happened?"

"Mary had died during the night."

"Oh, Adeline, I'm so sorry. You never told me."

"She wasn't the only one, you know, we lost a number of nurses that year."

"That must have been very difficult for all of you."

"Yes, it was tragic. It was one of the hardest things to come to terms with. I'm so grateful the war ended quickly after that brutal winter."

"Me, too, let's hope there will never be another war."

"I'll drink to that!"

"How about dreaming on that? Come to bed, darling. It's getting late. Let's try going back to sleep. Perhaps you'll be able to sleep a bit more peacefully now.

"Okay, I'll try, Harry."

Adeline kissed her husband *goodnight* for the second time that night. She slept deeply and dreamt.

Chapter Seven

∾

April, 1918
Stationary Hospital #16
Le Treport, France

When they are put to the test,
Even angels have to rest.

They had hibernated in their frozen trenches all winter long but when the frost thawed on the hedgerows, they felt a stinging sensation seep into their bones as they began to move once again. When they crept out of their icy furrows, the craving to fight trickled back into their souls. The battle on *no man's land* resumed with one skirmish in the early spring, as though it had never stopped during the frosty winter.

By summer, the fighting on the front intensified and continued with earnest into the fall. With each battle, the Allies strengthened their hold as they trudged deeper into France. However the price they paid for their wins was tolled in human lives. For as the combat escalated, so did the number of casualties.

During those summer months, there was no rest for those caring for the wounded. Convoys arrived at Le Treport every day, sometimes twice a day. There was no scheduled time for their arrival. They came in the early morning, the late afternoon or in the middle of the night. There was hardly enough time to clean and bed the injured before another convoy followed closely behind. The soldiers arrived on stretchers or were carried on the backs of the medics, piggyback style. Those who could still walk, hopped and limped in, leaning heavily on their walking sticks and each other. They came with their heads, chests and abdomens wrapped in bloodied bandages or with their limbs firmly secured and positioned to prevent movement.

Soldiers arrived scarred and scratched, broken and battered, dizzy and dazed. Some looked right through the medics and didn't respond to their questions. "Shell-shocked", they called it. They had shrapnel and bullet holes in every part of their bodies. One platoon leader lost the tip of his pinky finger. He said it was shot right off in mid-air when he signaled to the squad under his command. Although it bled profusely, he insisted that he was returning to the front to fight when it healed.

"Junky *Jerries* got the wrong finger, they did. They should have aimed for my trigger finger."

When the surgical theatre tent was filled to capacity, the medical officers had no choice but to intervene on the ward because lead and metal from shrapnel could not linger in a man's flesh or infection would set in. After digging into a leg wound in search of a spent bullet, the doctor looked for shreds of fabric from the soldiers' uniforms that often became embedded in the soft tissue of their muscles with the impact of the bullet. There were times when all that was left to do was to bring in the mini-guillotine that the French had designed for swift amputations. When the nurse asked what would become of the severed limbs, the R.A.M.C. orderly assured her that they would be buried in the cemetery on the hill. She didn't believe him.

Hardly a cry of pain was ever heard during these horrific procedures. They were a strong and stoic bunch of boys who earned the title of *men of war*. During a surgery or debridement, they never complained. However, if the problem was a wood splinter embedded in a thumb, there were howls of torture.

Both the injured and the ill came, and there were never enough beds for all of them. The nurses fretted about laying the stretchers directly on the ground because they knew the mice and ants would be attracted to the pungent smell of infection. Later the nurses would have to splash water on the wounds when they found them covered in a brown layer of ants. The up, ambulatory patients were placed in chairs in the middle of the tent. Those who were sick with *trench fever*, tetanus and *blue pus infections* were labeled *S-Is*, seriously ill while the *D-Is*, the dangerously ill patients, were isolated in smaller tents. The orderlies were quick at assembling pup tents to separate the dying soldiers from the others. The *D-Is* were designated for one-on-one nursing care but there was never enough nurses to care for them. Often one nurse watched over two or three soldiers, holding their hands, wetting their brows and praying over them as they died in her arms.

They received no official news from headquarters about how the war was progressing. There were no regular newspapers available to outline the details and outcome of each battle. The only news they heard came from the mouths of the boys returning from the front.

"Hundreds were wounded, nurse. They lay there for hours. If they weren't dead already, they died soon after."

"There wasn't anything any of us could do. One guy, we called him *Jack O'Lantern*, climbed out of the trench to save his trench-foot buddy.

He dodged the machine guns and dragged the soldier back to us only to get a bullet in his chest as he climbed down the ladder. He died in my arms. When we examined his buddy, we found that he had died out on the field hours before."

There were weeks when everyone worked through the night and into the next day for thirty-six or more hours at a stretch, allowing only a few hours to wash, eat and sleep. After months at that pace, the Nursing Superintendent knew that her nurses could not continue in that manner and decided to do something. One afternoon in early fall, she sat on her bunk and devoted the next two hours to intense concentration. The end product was a creative and ambitious maneuver of the master schedule and a mandate that every nurse and *VAD* would have a full twenty-four hours of restorative rest after every six days of work. In addition, she arranged for the local village girls to prepare and bring breakfast in bed to those having a rest day.

Although she protested, Nurse Adeline was included on the rest schedule. Her supervisor insisted that every staff member was to comply with her mandate.

So on her assigned day off, Adeline woke up after a restless sleep and was served breakfast in bed. Margaux, the village girl, delivered a three-egg omelet that her mother had made with the mushrooms she picked in the forest. On the plate, she added a boiled potato, a baguette of French bread and a jelly jar filled with cherry-apple jam.

After she ate every morsel of her precious breakfast omelet, Adeline finished off the entire jar of jam, licking her spoon until the glass bottle was empty. Then she lay back down on her pillow and relaxed into a deep and heavy slumber and dreamt of home.

Chapter Eight

～

February 1926
Nativity Settlement House
Williamsburg, Brooklyn

The angels soothe a fiery ear,
And put at ease a mother's fear.

"Why do you think you are dreaming of the war after all these years?" Angie asked Adeline. The two women were quietly talking in the tiny back room office at Nativity House.

"I don't know for certain, perhaps I'm worried about baby Henry going off to war. The *tommies* were so young when they enlisted."

"Do the dreams linger with you all day long?" Angie asked.

"No, if I remember them when I wake up, I feel grateful that the war is over. I try not to think about them during the day."

"Perhaps that's the reason why you're having these dreams. You aren't allowing yourself to have your memories."

"Harry agrees with you. He says that if I discuss the dreams, I might come to terms with the past."

"He's probably right to encourage you to bring them out into the light of day. You never shared your war stories with me when we were living in the nurses' residence cottage on Ellis Island. I'm glad you are now. Were you in much danger while you were caring for the wounded soldiers?"

"No, I wasn't working at a *Dressing Station* or a *Casualty Clearing Station.*"

"What are those?"

"The *Dressing Stations* were the mobile medical units located closest to the fighting. Many of them were only yards away from the trenches. They were the *triage* and first aid stations. The wounded would be carried to them directly from the front through trenches and underground tunnels."

"Were they then brought to a hospital?" Angie asked.

"No, the hospitals were in the villages, farther north, far from the fighting. You see, there was a chain of medical stops. Convoys could take the wounded only a short distance before they were forced to stop, rest and give care. All the stops through France led north to the port of Calais in order to take the boys across the English Channel to England."

"Much like a Pony Express."

"More like the Underground Railroad with designated rest stops."

"So what was the next stop?"

"At a *Dressing Station*, a soldier would be given first aid and sent back to the field or he went on to a *C.C.S.*"

"What's a *C.C.S.*?"

"Oh, *C.C.S.* is short for *Casualty Clearing Station.* They were often huge affairs that could serve almost a thousand men. They were situated a mile or two from the front...close enough for the limping wounded to reach them on foot and the badly injured to be carried on stretchers. Soldiers who were fit to travel joined a transit convoy of twenty to thirty horse wagons. Often the *S-Is*, the severely ill soldiers, were put on river barges to float to a neighboring village where a hospital was located."

"Why didn't they use automobiles?"

"Only a handful of automobiles were available during the war. The convoys carried the wounded and all the supplies that were needed to make the tedious trip to the next hospital. They had to carry water, medicine and food, enough for both the men and the horses."

"Then what?"

"The convoys delivered the sick and wounded soldiers to the next hospital along the route until they reached the town of Calais. The trip could sometimes take weeks."

"I can't imagine being wounded and having to travel on a horse cart."

"Yes and sometimes the trip aggravated their condition."

"In what way?"

"A broken bone could move, sever a tendon and cause a hemorrhage. That happened frequently until we started to use splints to immobilize a bone."

"What's the difference between a base hospital and a what?

"A *Stationary Tent Hospital*..." Adeline took a deep breath and asked. "Angie, do you really want to hear all this?"

"Yes, it's interesting and it's a part of your life that you've never shared with me before. Please, go on. I'm listening."

"Okay, a base hospital would be located in an actual building. The military took over an existing hospital in a city or they converted a country chateau into a hospital. The smaller villages used their town halls and hotels as hospitals. When more hospitals were needed, stationary tents were assembled to serve as medical hospitals."

"I remember you told me that you worked in a converted hotel in the village of La Roche Guyon," Angie added.

"Yes," Adeline continued. "When I first arrived in France, I was stationed at a hotel hospital for three months, working with the mustard gas recoveries. However when the Yanks took over the English tented hospital in Le Treport, I was transferred there. As the Assistant Superintendent of Nurses, I was put in charge of the *VAD*s."

"The military speak a different language. What's a *VAD*?"

"*VAD*s are volunteer ladies from England with no professional training. *V-A-D* stands for voluntary aide detachment. They were nursing aides. Well, better than aides. You see, over the years, the British sisters trained them to be skilled military nurses. Remember the Great War had been raging for three years before the United States entered it. When America entered the war, the Brits transferred the management of some of their hospitals to the American forces. The British left half of their *VAD* contingent with us at Le Treport. I was in charge of transitioning them."

Dr. Abe walked into the tiny backroom office to find the two women deep in conversation. "Ah, here you are. I thought you both might be in here. Mrs. Moratelli is in the reception room."

Angie jumped up. "I'm sorry, Abe. I didn't realize it was two o'clock already."

"No, you're not late. Mrs. Moratelli is early. It's only five minutes to two. When she rang the bell, I let her in and asked her to take a seat. I told her that she would be our first official patient this afternoon. The sisters from Nativity School sent for her to bring Johnny into the clinic."

"What's wrong?"

"It's his ear. It may be infected. I'm going to take a look at it."

"I'll get him ready for you, Abe. Just give me a minute." As she hurriedly left the room, Angie straightened the skirt of her uniform.

Angie raced through the clinic to find Mrs. Moratelli patiently waiting in a reception room, reading to her two sons. Marghereta Moratelli was a young widow who had lost her husband to meningitis the year before. Still in her twenties, she appeared older than her age. Her dark brown hair was haphazardly tied back in a loose bun that was coming undone. Slouching down in her chair, she looked thin and frail.

Angie knew Marghereta was working hard to support her family. After her husband Michaelo died, Abe found work for the widow. She cleaned the offices of a dentist and an eye doctor on Graham Avenue after office hours. Impressed with her meticulous cleaning, both doctors hired Marghereta to tend to their mansion homes during the day.

Five-year-old Johnny-boy, Marghereta's youngest son, was stretched out on two chairs. He held his hand over his right ear and was moaning. When Marghereta looked up, Angie noticed dark circles under her eyes.

"You look weary, Mrs. Moratelli. Are the boys behaving?"

"Oh, yes, Miss Angie, they've been good as gold. Why, Mikey walked twenty blocks to come get me, almost a mile. The sisters sent him."

"Are you working too hard?"

"No, Miss Angie, it's not the work. It's the worry."

"Your little boy looks a little feverish. Come with me. The doctor is in the examination room. Let's have the doctor exam Johnny now and we can finish our talk after the visit."

"I'm worried, Nurse Angie. He looks so very sick. The sisters said he might have a fever."

Doctor Abe was ready to examine Johnny as they entered the room. Angie put a thermometer in the boy's mouth as her husband readied his stethoscope to listen to the boy's heart and lungs.

"One hundred and one," Angie announced as she shook down the thermometer before placing it in a metal emesis bowl. She opened the tin of metal otoscope tips that were soaking in alcohol and dried one off before placing it on the instrument and handing it to the doctor.

"As we suspected," Doctor Abe said after he looked at the inside of Johnny's ear with his otoscope. "This little fellow's ear is red hot. I'd like to take a look at his brother's ear, too, as long as he's here."

After the doctor examined both boys, he instructed Mrs. Moratelli to go home and put Johnny to bed. "Let him rest his ear on a hot-water bottle...not too hot...just warm...that will give him some relief. Don't put his ear directly on the rubber. Cover it with a cloth."

"Yes, I know, doctor."

"Give him plenty of liquids. Put a drop of hydrogen peroxide in his ear three times a day and at bedtime. Come back at the end of the week. I want to have another look at his ear in a few days."

"I can't bring him back this week, doctor. I have to work."

"We're open on Saturday. Can you come then?"

"Oh, yes, doctor. I'm off on Saturday afternoons. Does Mikey have an ear infection also?"

"No, Mikey's ear looks fine."

"I've got to get back to work to prepare dinner."

"Are they expecting you?"

"Yes, I'll put Johnny to bed and have Mikey watch him until I get home."

"May I offer a suggestion?" Angie asked. "How about we bed Johnny-boy down in our sick room? We'll look after him this afternoon so that Mikey can return to school."

"Would you do that?"

"Of course, Mrs. Moratelli, now come upstairs with me and let's get Johnny-boy settled. Then you can be on your way."

"Are you sure, Nurse Angie? I can't get back here until six."

"Absolutely, it's no problem at all."

At the sink, Angie filled three Dixie-cups with water. "Mikey, it looks like you could use a big glass of water before you return to school."

Mikey looked up at his mother. "Do I have to go back to school today, Ma?"

"Yes! Do as Nurse Angie says, drink your water."

"Mrs. Moratelli, would you like a drink, also? Here's one for Johnny-boy and one for you." Angie handed each of them a Dixie-cup filled with water.

"Thank you, Nurse Angie." Marghereta reached for the water and turned to her oldest son. "Off you go now, Mikey. There's an hour of school left. You go, get today's homework assignment and don't forget to bring home your math book in your schoolbag. Yesterday, you forgot it. I want you home right after school to check on Nona."

"Mikey can come here after school you know. Our new after-school center opened last month. I can sign up both boys. The sisters accompany them across the street. They walk them right up to our door after school."

"I don't know…"

"You look concerned. There's no charge to you. It's free to the families who live in the neighborhood."

"Oh, that would be wonderful but…"

Marghereta stopped in midsentence and stared at the nurse.

"What were you going to say, Mrs. Moratelli? Is there something bothering you?"

"It's not the money. It's my mother. The boys look after her until I can get home."

"Is she not feeling well?"

"Well enough, Nurse Angie, but she gets into trouble when she's left alone."

"In what way?"

"She's decided her job is to take the kitchen wallpaper off the wall bit by bit. She shredded a whole wall of wallpaper next to the breakfast table. The landlord warned me that if she doesn't stop, he will evict the lot of us. She's grouchy and ornery, too. Nothing pleases her. She gets mad when I tell her to do something. Oh yes, and she's always complaining about her bunions."

"Why don't you bring her in?"

"I can't, Nurse Angie. She has no shoes that fit."

"So she never goes out?"

"No, I take her to church and sometimes we sit in the park but only on nice days when it's sunny. She can't go out in the rain."

"Why is that?"

"It's because there are no shoes that fit her feet. She's needs a size-four shoe that is very wide. They don't make shoes that wide in a shoe size that small. I crocheted slippers for her. She wears them instead of shoes when we go out but they get dirty. I have to wash and scrub them every time we go out."

"Can you bring her in on a nice day, maybe on Saturday when you return with Johnny?"

"There's another problem I have with her. She won't wait a minute. She's even more fidgety than the boys. She gets antsy if she has to wait. I don't want to make a scene in this nice place."

"I will make every effort to take her right away. Better yet, I have an idea. What if I send our visiting nurse to your apartment? She could check up on her and examine her bunions. Would that help?"

"Oh, yes, Miss Angie, you could do that?"

"Of course, I will submit a referral for a home visit. Nurse O'Shaughnessy is assigned to Williamsburg on Tuesdays and Thursdays. She might be able to see your mother by the end of the week."

"She'll have to ring the landlady's bell. My mother won't answer the door to strangers."

"I will make note of that."

"Is there anything else I have to do?"

"Just take care of your boys and yourself, too. You go back to work now and don't worry about a thing. I'll look after your Johnny-boy and will handle everything."

Marghereta left Nativity House feeling a little lighter and standing a little taller. This was the first time someone had understood her difficult situation and had offered real help to unburden her of her many responsibilities. Since her husband Michaelo had died, she had been all alone with no one to turn to for help. Now the doctor and nurse were watching over her son and were sending a visiting nurse out to see her mother. Her husband always said, "Everything happens for a reason."

Marghereta smiled at the mental image she had of her husband Michaelo watching over them and leading them straight to the open doors of Nativity House.

Chapter Nine

≈

March 1926
Williamsburg, Brooklyn

In winter's snow and summer's heat,
The angels nurse from street to street.

Visiting Nurse Maureen O'Shaughnessy was grateful the day was mild and sunny. Only two days before, it had been so windy on Montrose Avenue that her navy-blue visiting nurse cap flew right off her head and landed in the middle of the cobblestone street. Luckily, a gentleman crossing the street at that exact moment lost no time in swooping down to catch her hat before it was run over by a streetcar. When he reached the sidewalk, he graciously delivered it to her in one piece.

Maureen spent the better part of the winter trudging through slush and snow, dodging rainstorms and fighting off freezing weather to visit her patients in the privacy of their home. For the first time in months, she delighted in the pleasure of working outdoors. The lovely day teased her with a hint of a remembrance that spring would soon be around the corner. Her uniform blue suit with its matching blue overcoat was all the outerwear she needed on this pleasant day. Even her black medicine bag was lighter without the emergency outer gear and umbrella she often carried in anticipation of inclement weather.

Maureen was one of Lillian Wald's visiting nurses from Henry Street Settlement House in the city. Two days a week, on Tuesdays and Thursdays, Maureen traveled to Brooklyn to care for the sick and elderly who were referred to her by the nurses at Nativity Settlement House and Health Clinic in Williamsburg, Brooklyn. Her daily schedule often included ten to twelve home visits. The visits ranged from a simple drop-in to check medications and vital signs to longer sessions, such as teaching family members how to reduce the spread of infection or instructing a new mother how to care for her infant.

Maureen enjoyed traveling to Brooklyn and working with the staff at Nativity House. She loved her work and put a hundred percent effort into everything she did for her patients. At first she wasn't thrilled to be assigned to Brooklyn. She thought the extra time traveling from the city would extend her workday but from her very first day, she knew the assignment was right for her. She had met her fiancé, Sam Goodwin, when she arrived at Nativity House to introduce herself to Nurse Angie, the nursing director at the clinic. On that afternoon, Dr. Goodwin's brother had come to pick up his mother. Sam was immediately attracted to Maureen and offered to drive Maureen to the Henry Street Settlement House at the end of the day.

Maureen looked down at her list of patients. She had one new patient, eighty-eight year old Carmela Tagliano, who lived with her widowed daughter in a second-floor walkup on Meserole Street. When Maureen arrived at the building, she rang the bell to Mrs. Tagliano's apartment but received no answer. After her second attempt to reach the woman inside, she checked her intake card and noted the instructions to ring the landlady's ground-floor-front apartment for assistance.

Rozalia Borkowski answered the bell. "Who's there?" she called out.

"Visiting Nurse O'Shaughnessy for Mrs. Tagliano. I was told you might be able to assist me."

"Wait right there."

Maureen waited for what seemed like an eternity until Mrs. Borkowski opened her window and looked out. "Just checking, Miss, to see if it was really you before I opened the door. People are always tricking me, trying to get into the building."

"Did Mrs. Moratelli speak to you about letting me in?"

"Yes, she did. You want to check on the old lady, right?"

"Yes, Mrs. Tagliano, she lives on the second floor."

"Stay put. I'll come get you."

Maureen patiently waited outside until the landlady unlocked the front door of the building.

"Come in, Miss. Follow me." Mrs. Borkowski continued to talk as Maureen followed her up a flight of stairs. "Glad someone's doing something about that old lady. She's ruining the apartment, you know. My Gleason got so angry when he saw what she did to the kitchen. He wanted to evict them all on the spot but I stopped him. I'm the one with the good heart, you know. I got to feeling sorry for Greta. I know she has her hands full with the boys and her mother and needs all the help she can get. She's a good girl...always pays the rent on time... works two jobs...never complains. So I say, 'Glee, at least they're not asking you to fix up the place. As long as they stay put, you don't have to do nothing, and the only wallpaper in the whole apartment is in the kitchen.' I convinced him to leave them alone for the time being but God only knows what that old woman will think up next to destroy the place. Here we are."

The landlady knocked on the door and waited. When she received no answer, she called out, "Carmela, it's me, Rosie. I'm coming in to see you. Don't be frightened, dear."

As the two women entered, they found Carmela Tagliano standing on a kitchen chair, industriously working on removing tiny bits of wallpaper.

"What are you doing, Carmela?"

"Nothing."

"Well, come down from that chair. You could fall."

"Yes, Mrs. Tagliano, it is very dangerous for you to be climbing on chairs," Maureen added.

"Who are you?"

"Carmela, this is Visiting Nurse O'Shaughnessy. She's come to see you. The doctor sent her to look at your feet."

"Oh, that's nice."

"How are you feeling today, Mrs. Tagliano?"

"As good as to be expected. My bunions are hurting."

Before Maureen could answer, the landlady interrupted. "Well, I'll leave you two alone for now. I'll be downstairs if you need me."

Maureen helped the elderly lady down from the chair and explained that she would examine her. The woman was happy to comply and appeared to enjoy the attention. She willingly showed Maureen her feet with bunions so large and swollen that they had pushed her big toes to the side at a sharp right angle. Both of her big toes were deformed and laid across and on top of her smaller toes.

"Your bunions appear to be swollen today. Are they always like this?"

"They are hurting more than usual."

Maureen completed her intake assessment on her new patient as she soaked Carmela's feet in warm soapy water, calmly talking to her and asking her questions. She cleaned between her toes and cut her overgrown toenails. "I heard that you don't have any shoes that fit your feet."

"Nothing fits right now. My daughter crocheted these slippers for me."

"Well, I'll have to look into finding you a pair of shoes so that you can go out. Would you like to come down to the settlement house some mornings?"

"Why would I go there?"

"They have activities for you and you could meet other people. Would you like that?"

"I don't know. I have to ask my daughter."

After Maureen massaged the woman's feet with medicated cream and was putting on her slippers, she heard a rumbling sound coming from the apartment above.

"What's that?" she asked.

"It's only the girls upstairs."

"What are they doing?"

"When they get a little bored, they put on their skates and skate in the house."

"Their mother lets them do that?"

"Oh, the mother is never around…works all day and is out all night."

"So the girls are left alone?"

"Most of the time, sometimes they come down to see me."

"Why aren't they in school today?"

"One of them had her tonsils out last month at the eye and ear clinic. The other one stays home with her to keep her company."

"Shouldn't they be in school by now?"

"I don't know. You have to ask Rosie about that."

Maureen knocked on the landlady's door as she was leaving the building. "I just wanted to tell you that I'm leaving now. I will be back next week."

"How did she look to you?" Rozalia asked.

"Her bunions are swollen. It may be due to an infection or a gout inflammation. I'd like to take her into the clinic for the doctor to have a look at her feet."

"Good luck with that, Miss."

"Mrs. Borkowski, I want to ask you about the girls who live on the third floor."

"Oh, those sweet things are always amusing themselves, playing at some one thing or another. They're no bother, no bother at all."

"Shouldn't they be in school today?"

"Little Hildie had her tonsils out and she's recuperating.

"Where's their mother?"

"She's out working. She works during the day and goes out in the evening."

"What do the girls do?"

"They take care of themselves and do a good job of it, too."

"How old are they?"

"Hildie is five. Hanna is seven."

"...And they are home alone all day and all evening?"

"Yes. Sometimes I check on them and give them something to eat, out of the goodness of my heart. I asked the woman how she can leave the little girls alone in the apartment all the time. She said, 'They're not alone, Rosie. They're with each other'."

"Yes, but…"

"Makes no sense to me but she says she's a good mother. She said she could have put them in the city orphanage but didn't. Truth is she takes care of them good enough. She comes home at five-thirty on the dot to feed them, but then off she goes at seven all perfumed and dolled up."

"Do the girls go to school?"

"Not right now but their mother said she will sign them up in September."

"What do they do in the summer?"

"They play. They think up all kinds of things to keep themselves amused. Sometimes they even visit the old lady. As I said, Miss, I don't mind them. They're good girls."

"Do you think maybe we can get the girls enrolled at some of the activities at the settlement house this summer?"

"That would be nice. I gotta go now, Miss. What was your name again?"

"Maureen O'Shaughnessy."

"Good talking to you."

"Yes, nice meeting you, Mrs. Borkowski. You've been most helpful. I'll be back next week."

"Well now, you go enjoy the rest of this lovely day."

"You, too, and thank you for your assistance."

Chapter Ten

April 1926
New York City

When she presented her request,
His challenge put her to the test.

Leonora Bartoli woke up with an idea. Without wasting a second, she jumped out of bed and rushed into the kitchen in her silk nightgown. "Millie, I noticed the chi-chi beans were soaking last night. Are you making them for dinner?"

"Yes, Miss, I'm boiling them now. This is a fine way to greet me, Miss Leonora, coming in here not dressed and not even taking the time to say a *good-morning* to your Millie."

"Oh, I am sorry, Millie. How rude of me. It's just that…"

"Just what, Miss?"

"I had an idea to surprise Papa. I would like to make the chi-chi beans for Papa today. It's his favorite dish."

"It's his favorite dish, that's for sure, and he'll be complaining if it's not made to his liking. Do you even know how to make the chi-chis?" Millie asked.

"I've watched you a hundred times."

"Well, I suggest you watch me one more time. We'll make it together."

"No, I want to tell Papa I cooked it all by myself."

"...and why's that, Miss?"

"I have a favor to ask him."

Millie looked toward heaven. "I smell trouble brewing, already. Please, Lord, don't make me a part of it." Then she added, "He'll be working himself into a lather if he doesn't like your cooking."

"No, Millie, he won't get angry."

"Want to wager a bet?" Millie asked.

"Millie, he won't get mad. He will be proud of me for preparing his favorite dish."

"That's what you think. We've all seen him hooting and hollering when his food is not prepared to his liking." Millie made the sign of the cross, "...and, God forbid, if his food is too hot. The man never stops to check. He shoves it into his mouth and blames me for burning him. Last week, he came barreling into the kitchen and threw his dish of veal stew right into the garbage...dish and all...said it tasted like vinegar. Do you want to take a chance that he will do that with your cooking, Miss Leonora?"

"I can do it, Millie," Leonora insisted and stamped her foot on the linoleum floor.

"Don't be starting to get a temper on me like your Papa. One with a temper in this house is enough, isn't it? Before I turn over my chi-chi beans to you, tell me how you're gonna make 'em."

"Okay, you cut up the pancetta and fry it in olive oil with an onion and garlic. Then you add two cups of the garbonza beans, a little of the broth, oregano, salt and pepper. You make the ditali pasta separately, drain it and add the chi-chi bean mixture. It's as simple as that."

"Okay, Missy. After you get dressed, you can give it your best, but I'll be standing here watching you every step of the way. There'll be hell to pay if he doesn't take a liking to it."

Eugenio Bartoli expected his food cooked the way he liked it with no changes, no substitutions and no creative modifications. He wanted his chicken cutlets thin and crispy, his sausages evenly browned and his pasta al dente. He liked his tiny pastina thick, his oatmeal firm and his dinner rolls soft and fresh. If Millie wanted to experiment, she could do it with someone else's food, not his. He felt he had earned the right to demand perfection. After all, perfection is what he gave his customers.

Eugenio Bartoli made hand-crafted custom shoes and sold them to the city's wealthiest clients in New York. His shoe store was centrally located in the fashionable Upper East Side of Manhattan in the building that he owned and lived in with his family.

As a young boy, Eugenio had emigrated from Naples after completing his apprenticeship as a shoemaker. Upon his arrival in New York, he settled downtown among his friends, *paisans,* Napolitano countrymen. There he made shoes in the evening in his small tenement apartment. He sold the shoes from a pushcart during the day. After three years of struggling, Eugenio began to explore store locations throughout the city. During his search, he observed that wealthy people owned more than one pair of shoes. He decided, right there and then, that he would sell his top-quality shoes to the city's uptown elite. From that time on, he saved every cent he earned and used his meager savings to rent a small storefront. As word of mouth about his craftsmanship spread, his business grew. Thirty years later, Eugenio Bartoli was a prosperous businessman who made the best shoes in the city.

He refused to have his daughter work, not at his store and not for another employer. He felt that would be a bad reflection on his ability to support his family. Leonora had pleaded with her father until he agreed to allow her to volunteer at the Nativity Settlement House helping immigrant families.

At noon each day, Eugenio closed his store to eat lunch with his wife and daughter. Leonora could hear him slowly beginning to climb the three flights of stairs, stopping at each landing to catch his breath until he reached the family's top-floor apartment. Eugenio came in the apartment, kissed his wife and sat down at the dining room table.

"Mama, where's Leonora?" he asked.

"Here I am, Papa," Leonora called out. "I'm coming," she said as she carefully carried a piping-hot bowl of chi-chi beans and ditali pasta to the table without spilling a drop.

"Where's Millie?"

"In the kitchen, Papa. I have a surprise for you. I made the chi-chi beans today."

Eugenio looked surprised. "You made this? Let me have a taste."

"Be careful, Papa, blow on it. It's hot."

"I know-a it's hot. I blow."

Everyone sat at the table and didn't say a word as Eugenio picked up his spoon and tasted the dish of pasta.

"Ummm...," he said as he took another spoonful. "Not-a bad, not-a bad at all, in fact, tell Millie that you might be cooking her out of a job-a."

"You really like it, Papa?"

Leonora waited until he finished his dish of chi-chi beans. Then she said, "Papa, I have a favor to ask of you. There is a very elderly lady in Williamsburg. Her bunions are so big that she has no shoes to wear."

"Can she pay for new shoes?"

"No, that's the problem."

"I don't do charity shoes, Leonora. You know what-a I say: 'charity begins at home'. If I do for one, they all find out and come begging to me for handouts."

"She's from Napoli, your hometown, a *paisan*. She has no shoes and can't go outside."

"I ask-a you. Am I supposed to feel-a sorry?"

"Dr. Goodwin said he would pay for them if you give him a good price."

"Out of the question, I don't take money from the poor settlement house people. What would they think of me?"

"Can you do it for me?"

"For free?"

"Please, Papa, please."

"Okay, I will make them because she's a *paisan* but only on one condition. You must never tell anyone who made them. I don't want one word to get out. Then everyone will be asking me for charity shoes."

Leonora leaped up from her chair and hugged her father. "Thank you, Papa. Thank you."

"One hand washes the other, daughter. Now, you must do a favor for me."

"What, Papa? Anything!"

"Mama is going to invite the Rossi family here to our house next month. Mr. Rossi has a nice-a son, very handsome He wants-a to meet you. You do this for me. You put on a pretty dress and be-a nice to the boy."

"…But Papa, he's so fat."

"That's because his father owns a busy Italian restaurant and they make very good food."

"I'm not going to marry him if that's what you are thinking."

"Who said anything about marriage? You just-a have to be-a nice-a. You can do that for me, right?"

"Yes, Papa. I can do that. Let me have your dish and I will bring you your dessert."

"Did you make-a that, too?"

"No, Millie did."

Leonora carried the dirty dishes into the kitchen. When she put them down on the kitchen counter, Millie asked. "Well, how did it go? Did you get what you wanted?"

"Yes, Millie, but I have to meet Mr. Rossi's son as a favor to Papa."

"Do you mean that little fat boy whose father owns the restaurant around the corner?" Millie asked.

"Yes, he's the one but he's all grown up and not a little boy any-more," Leonora chuckled. "Although he still is chubby, isn't he, Millie?"

"Fat as a hippo…and that's okay with you?"

"No, of course not, but Papa says 'one hand washes the other'. He'll do a favor for me if I do a favor for him."

"What about your boyfriend, Alfonso?"

"How do you know about Alfonso?"

"I may have been born in the old country, but Millie's no fool. I can see what goes on downstairs every day. What will you tell Alfonso?"

"I don't know, Millie. I will have to think of something fast."

Chapter Eleven

May 1918
Stationary Hospital #16
Le Treport, France

Decisions made and followed through
Her orders dictate what she should do.

VAD Penelope Gibbons nervously rang the bell outside the administrative tent of Le Treport Camp. Assistant Superintendent Adeline Ferme' had summoned her for a private conference earlier in the day.

Because she knew the subject of their conversation would be a sensitive one, Adeline preferred to not sit behind her desk. Instead, she invited the *VAD* to sit down next to her near the fire. The two women sat side by side for a moment, listening to the crackle of the fire, before Adeline spoke.

"You know that I am required to dismiss you, Miss Gibbons."

Penelope could not look at her. Instead, she looked toward the fire. "Please, Sister."

"Call me Miss Ferme'. How long have you been stationed here at Le Treport?"

"Three years…"

"Isn't it time to go home?" Adeline asked.

"I can't go back to England, Miss. Please, you can't send me back, not like this."

"How far along are you, dear?"

"Three months, I think."

"...And you managed to keep it a secret all this time?"

"Yes."

"You understand I have no choice in this matter."

"Please don't send me home," the young girl begged.

"Surely, Miss Gibbons, you were aware of the rules. You can't continue to serve in your condition."

"I am not sick or anything."

"You are in a fragile state. You must think of your baby."

"I am. I didn't mean to get pregnant, Miss Ferme', but I did. I want this baby. I want you to know I'm a good woman. Sergeant Kingsley and I were attracted to each other but we never did anything about it. It was only that one night, the night before he was transferred when we said our goodbyes. The next day, he left for the front. Yesterday, I learned that he was shot. He's at a *C.C.S.* now. Please let me stay until he comes in with his convoy."

"It could be weeks before he comes through to our camp, if at all. We have no guarantee that his convoy will stop at this hospital site."

"I'll take that chance. This baby is all I have left of him. I am begging you. If I go back, they will force me to...."

"Who would?" Adeline asked.

"My parents, you see they have their reputation to consider. My father is a barrister. They will see to it that my situation is corrected."

"I am sorry, my dear."

"Don't call me *dear* when you are going to do this to me."

"I'm not doing this to you. Believe me. It's the rules."

"Can't you break the rules this one time? I'm begging you."

"No, Miss Gibbons, I cannot."

"I am not returning to Britain," Penelope announced.

"What will you do?" Adeline asked.

"I will run away," Penelope said defiantly as she stood up and ran out of the tent.

Adeline ran after the girl and called out. "Where are you going? Come back, Penelope! Please come back!"

Adeline followed Penelope until she lost sight of her. Adeline continued in the direction of the ocean until she saw Penelope running along the white cliffs toward the water.

"Stop, Penelope. Please, stop!"

Penelope ignored Adeline's frantic calls as she ran straight off the cliff into the raging water below.

Chapter Twelve

~

April 1926
Nativity Settlement House
Williamsburg, Brooklyn

He planned his course. His path was clear,
But fate stepped in to interfere.

"Adeline, how terrible! Did Penelope die?" Angie asked Adeline.

The nurses were sitting in the reception room, talking quietly after the Nativity House clinic had closed for the evening.

"No, it was a dream, remember."

"What happened to her?"

"She returned to England when she was discharged from military service."

"What became of her sergeant?"

"Three weeks after Penelope left, Sergeant Kingsley arrived at our base camp. He was part of an incoming convoy. He came with an infected gunshot wound to his left clavicle. It was touch-and-go for days. The doctors took him to surgical theatre twice for debridement. While he was recovering I visited him. I told him about Penelope...that she was pregnant and that she was upset when I sent her home. He was overjoyed with the news of the baby and was glad that Penelope was safely at home with her parents. From that point on, he seemed to heal faster than usual. It took us only another week to stabilize him. He wanted to be strong enough to return to England. He was determined to leave, find Penelope and marry her as soon as he was fit to travel...

"After the orderlies put him on the train to Calais, I boarded the stretcher car to bid him good-bye and wish him a safe journey. He was happy that he was healing and he would soon be reunited with Penelope. The whole camp was rooting for them."

"A romantic cinema ending..."

"I wish it were. Unfortunately, that's not what happened..."

"What happened, Adeline?"

"Days later, we learned that the ferry the sergeant was on was hit by a torpedo. Sergeant Kingsley didn't survive."

"Oh, no! What happened to Penelope? Did she have the baby?"

"I don't know. I never heard. I wrote her but I never heard back from her."

"Maybe it was the fault of the mail delivery system."

"No, the mail was being delivered. Many of the *tommies* wrote to me when they arrived home, thanking me and sending me pictures of their sweethearts and their families. We corresponded regularly. I know they received my letters because they wrote back again."

"I hope Penelope had a little boy who looked just like her sergeant."

"I don't know. A year later, I had returned to my job at Ellis Island Hospital and lost contact with her."

"Oh my, that's the saddest love story ever."

"I know," Adeline sighed and put her head down. When she looked up, there were tears in her eyes. "Oh Angie, it was the war. That's only one tragic love story. There were so many others."

Chapter Thirteen

❧

April 1926
Nativity Settlement House
Williamsburg, Brooklyn

The heart is filled with sorrow.
There will never be tomorrow.

Nurse Angie Goodwin had positioned her desk in the Nativity House reception room so that she would have both a clear view through the bay windows to the street outside and a good look at the front door as people entered the clinic.

Angie heard the shouting on the street long before she saw the four women frantically running toward the settlement house. One woman carried a bundle in her arms. Three other women followed behind, wheeling their baby carriages and racing to catch up with her. Suspecting that something was terribly wrong, Angie flew into action. She jumped up from her desk and ran to the examination station where she found her husband, Dr. Abe.

"Come quick, Abe. There seems to be a problem outside."

Abe Goodwin dropped the papers in his hand and followed his wife into the reception room. They reached the front door as the woman entered.

"Help! Help! Please, help me, Doctor. Please," the woman screamed frantically.

Dr. Abe stretched out both arms to the mother as she handed him her baby. He ran into the examination room with the baby and put him down on the table.

Leonora and Adeline, who were teaching an English class in the room next door, heard the screams and rushed into the reception room. Not knowing what to do, the women in the class followed them.

The mother of the baby collapsed into Adeline's arms, sobbing. "My baby, my baby," she cried.

Everyone in the room was shouting so loud that it was difficult to understand what had happened.

"We were all sitting outside."

"The babies were in their carriages."

"Trixie went upstairs to get drinks for us."

"Nellie said she was getting thirsty."

With the mention of her name, Nellie began to moan. "Oh, my baby! My baby! Whatever will I do?"

"It'll be all right, Nellie," one woman said, putting her hand on Nellie's shoulder in an attempt to soothe her. "The doctor has him now. He will be able to do something."

Angie put her hands up to quiet the crowd. "Please, please, everyone, try to calm down. We need to know what happened."

Adeline added, "One at a time, if you would, please tell us what happened." She turned to the mother of the baby and asked, "Can you tell us what happened?"

The mother dropped down on her knees and rocked back and forth on the floor.

"She's in shock," one woman whispered.

Adeline turned to Angie. "Go ahead, Angie. Abe may need your help. I'll take care of things out here."

Angie joined her husband. Dr. Abe had taken the baby's blankets off and had positioned the baby on his forearm. He held the baby's head in his hands as he firmly tapped the child's back in a careful attempt to clear his airway and stimulate a breath.

"I thought something might be caught in his airway, but...oxygen, Angie."

Angie hurried to the green oxygen tank and rolled it to the examination table. In one swift movement, she turned it on and put the nozzle near the baby's face while her husband listened for a heartbeat with his stethoscope.

The baby lay still...lifeless...blue-gray...not breathing.

"Nothing," he said. "Not a sound."

Adeline entered the examination room with a report. "The women said they found the baby not breathing. He had been sleeping peacefully on his tummy all morning. They were all sitting together outside, talking and enjoying the sunshine...

"The mother is Nell O'Donegan. It was almost eleven when one of the ladies said she was thirsty and went upstairs to her apartment to get drinks for everyone. After Nell drank her lemonade, she checked on her son, intending to take a few of the blankets off him. That's when she found him, not moving. They panicked and didn't know what to do."

"How long ago was that?"

"I don't know but it was a while before they came up with the idea to bring the baby to us. Then they ran the whole six blocks."

"Oh, dear," Angie sighed.

"So we don't know when the baby stopped breathing?" Abe asked.

"No, only that it was sometime after eleven."

"That was thirty-five minutes ago."

The three caregivers continued their attempts to stimulate the baby. However the tiny baby remained unresponsive on the table.

Finally, after what seemed like an eternity, Dr. Abe asked, "Angie, what time is it?"

Angie whispered, "...eleven forty-two."

"I have to pronounce the little one." He leaned over the examination table and put his head down as if he was praying. Angie's heart broke to see him so helpless. "Please, Angie. Please bring in Mrs. O'Donegan. I must tell her that her baby has died."

Chapter Fourteen

Nativity Settlement House
Williamsburg, Brooklyn

From deep within and far below,
A dream still burns and is aglow.

After Doctor Abe pronounced baby boy Francis O'Donegan, Jr. and called the police department and...

After Officer Gallagher arrived and filled out the application for the death certificate, listing the cause of death as *UNK*, unknown, and...

After Father Mahoney was summoned and blessed both the baby and his mother and after he gathered the women in the reception room and led them in prayer and...

After the baby's father, Francis O'Donegan, was called and arrived within minutes. He had been sleeping in his apartment six blocks away after working the night shift at the bagel factory on the other side of Brooklyn and...

After Sam Goodwin, Abe's brother, the undertaker, came and explained the burial procedure to Mr. and Mrs. O'Donegan and...

After Doctor Abe and his brother, Sam, left Nativity House to drive the O'Donegans to their apartment and...

After Adeline dismissed the women in her English class and went to assist the volunteers preparing for the afterschool program and...

ANGELS IN BROOKLYN

After all the women fed their babies and returned home to prepare dinner for their husbands, thankful their babies were still breathing and safe in their baby carriages and...

After all the commotion at Nativity Settlement House settled, Angie sat alone at her reception room desk, thinking, pondering and wondering.

She asked herself only one question: *Why would a strong, healthy baby suddenly die?*

Angie had hoped and prayed for a child of her own. She had lost her own baby in the early stages of her pregnancy many years before. It was difficult for her at the time. She had felt the movement of the infant inside her only the week before her loss. She wondered what it must be like to lose an infant after carrying him, birthing him and breastfeeding him, only to have him suddenly slip away in an instant. The loss of a child was one of the greatest losses a woman would ever experience. Such a loss would stay with a mother forever.

Angie had many questions.

Why did some young infants die suddenly for no apparent reason? Could the cause be a heart defect or other ailment that wasn't detected at birth but surfaced months later? Did the baby stop breathing because of suffocation or did the infant die from hyperthermia? The women reported that the baby was sleeping soundly on his tummy and looked peaceful and comfortable when they last checked him. The day had been getting progressively warmer and the sun was shining on their side of the street. Did the carriage top protect the baby from the sun? Did the temperature inside the baby carriage rise to quickly?

Angie's thoughts were interrupted by the shrill sound of the after-school dismissal whistle at Nativity Catholic School.

She looked outside to see the children gathering in the schoolyard across the street. At the public schools the children were dismissed when the school bell rang, the universal signal that school was over for the day. However, at Nativity Catholic School, there was a dismissal procedure that was religiously followed each and every day.

Angie watched as the children assembled with their class. The older children were instructed to line up on the left side of the court-yard while the younger children gathered on the right. The children who attended the afterschool program at the settlement house formed a straight line in back of them, waiting for Sister Mary Geraldine to walk them across the street. Sister would come for them after all the elementary school classes were dismissed.

With the tinkle of a handbell, the procession began. The fifth-grade class marched along Johnson Avenue until they reached Graham Avenue while the kindergarten class marched in the opposite direction toward Humboldt Street. Once they arrived at the corner, they waited until their teacher clicked on the small tin clicker she held under her habit apron. That was their signal to disperse. After them, the six-graders left the schoolyard, followed by the children in the seventh and eighth grades. Each class followed the other in this orderly progression.

The mothers who met their children after school had been instructed to wait at the corner of Johnson Avenue and Humboldt Street. If a mother was waiting for an older child, the older child was required to cross the street and walk back to the Humboldt Street corner.

Many of the younger children were met by their mothers. However not all the children had parents waiting for them when they came out of class. Some scattered away unsupervised. Most went straight home while some lingered, waiting for their older sisters and brothers to walk them home. When they had a penny in their pockets, they stopped at Maryann's Candy Store to pick a penny candy from her colorful jars of sweets. If they had a few pennies more, they congregated around Pete, the Pretzelman, to buy a warm, soft pretzel from the old baby carriage he used as a pushcart. In the spring, they would line up at the side window of Milano's Bakery to buy lemon ice served in a pleated papercup.

Angie usually delighted in observing the school dismissal procedure but she found it troubling that, once again, she spotted a young man lingering across the street. He was neatly dressed in simple, clean clothes, wearing a tan sweater and pressed trousers. The cap he wore covered his eyes and made it difficult to see his face. He didn't look like the suspicious type. However what aroused Angie's suspicion was that this was not the first time that she had noticed the man. He wasn't there every day but she saw him once or twice a week. Often he arrived minutes before the dismissal whistle blew. At first, she thought he was a father of one of the schoolchildren who might be too embarrassed to wait with the group of mothers at the corner.

She wondered: *Was he waiting or watching?*

Angie worried about the children going home unsupervised. She knew that some had to care for their younger siblings who were home alone during the day. One ten-year-old was required to walk a half mile to pick up her baby brother from her aunt's house. There was also a little kindergarten girl who waited at the corner for her older sister who attended the public school a mile away. What if this young man was identifying the stragglers? Perhaps she should talk to Officer Gallagher to alert the policemen on the neighborhood beat.

Angie was deep in thought when Leonora walked through the reception room on her way home. "I didn't mean to startle you, Nurse Angie. I just wanted to say *goodnight*."

"Leonora, do you have a few minutes? Do you want to discuss what happened before you leave?" Angie asked.

"No, I'm okay, Nurse Angie. Adeline explained things to us a little while ago. I have to run. I thought I would stop at church this evening and light a candle for the parents."

"That's thoughtful, Leonora. Thank you for all your work today."

"I'll be back tomorrow, Nurse Angie."

When Leonora opened the door to leave, Abe walked in.

"Hi, Doctor Abe."

"Hi, Leonora, are you leaving?"

"Yes, I've got to go. I promised my father I'd be home before five."

"Best be on your way, Leonora. If you catch the three-thirty street-car into the city, you should arrive on time."

"Good evening to you, Doctor," Leonora said as she closed the door behind her.

"How did it go, Abe?" Angie asked.

"As well as can be expected, I suppose. The parents are still trying to absorb what happened. They had so many questions for me. Angie, it breaks my heart not to have answers for them."

"I can't even imagine what it must be like for them to experience such a tragedy so unexpectedly."

"Mrs. O'Donegan told me she had a difficult time getting pregnant. She's worried she may not be able to have another child."

"What did you tell her?"

"One step at a time…that was all I could say. I felt so helpless. She is blaming herself. She thinks she did something wrong."

"I know, most mothers do in these situations. One minute her baby is alive and the next instant his fragile life slips away from her."

"If only they could have reached us in time."

"I wish we knew what caused this to happen."

"Me, too, Angie, research suggests that it could be a number of things. There's some documentation on the subject. Someday we'll find an answer. I hope this doesn't happen again but if it does, perhaps we should keep a record of our cases."

"Yes, we should document everything we know about the child."

"In a week or two, let's interview the mother. Ask her if she was breastfeeding or bottle feeding."

"She mentioned she had a difficult time breastfeeding and started to feed the baby from a bottle last month."

"We should find out what she was giving the baby."

"Do you think that could make a difference?"

"Perhaps or perhaps not, but we should gather all the information we can about the baby. We may discover patterns. We should find out how the baby was sleeping and eating and if the baby had colic. If we could encourage the parents to bring their babies in to us regularly when they're well, we would have this information on record."

"Oh, Abe, before I forget, the reporter from *The Brooklyn Bugle* called. He is interested in writing an article about the clinic. He wants to interview us."

"Really? When?"

"He said, 'as soon as possible'. I told him I would call him to set up a date and time after I discussed it with you."

"Let's do it, Angie. The clinic can always use good publicity."

"I agree. Abe, there's another thing."

"What's that, Angie?"

"I wanted to ask you if you ever noticed a man waiting across the street."

"What man?"

"I've seen a young man waiting across the street a number of times, but he doesn't stand with the mothers. Come, he's there now. Take a look and tell me what you think."

When they walked to the window and looked out, the man had disappeared. Angie looked puzzled. "He was there a minute ago."

"He must have been waiting for one of the schoolchildren."

"Yes, I suppose."

"Call me if you see him again, Angie." Abe took his wife into his arms and kissed her. He asked, "Are you very upset about what happened today?"

"Yes, of course..."

"I am, also. Angie, how about we have dinner out this evening, perhaps Ricci's?"

"Good idea, I think a walk to Ricci's and dinner out might be what we need after a day like today."

Angie and Abe weren't able to leave Nativity House until after seven o'clock. The sun was beginning to set as they walked to Ricci's Italian Restaurant.

"It's a lovely night, Angie"

"Yes, the weather is getting warmer."

"Soon it will be summer."

"After everything that's happened today, it's hard to imagine that this evening can be so peaceful."

"I know you're upset about the baby, especially when we're planning to have a baby of our own."

"Yes, I was thinking of that today. I can't imagine what I would do if I were to lose a child."

"Well, first things first, we haven't been blessed with a child as yet."

"Yes, I know but I can't help worrying and wondering."

"Wondering, what?"

"What if we ever had to deal with a challenge like that?"

Abe stopped walking and looked at his wife. "Angie, I believe that together we can handle anything that comes our way."

Then Abe took his wife in his arms and kissed her.

Chapter Fifteen

May 22, 1926
The Brooklyn Bugle
Front Page Article

A Settlement House in Brooklyn
By Clarence Wilkins

At first glance, the house at 148 Johnson Avenue looks like all the brick row houses on Johnson Avenue. However, upon closer inspection, you will notice two brass plates on the green door. The larger one is engraved with the words: Nativity Settlement House and Health Clinic. The other reads: All are welcome.

Upon entering, you will find yourself in the lively reception room which is the hub of all settlement house activity. This is the place where neighbors come together to sign up for the health clinic, register their children for the afterschool program or enroll in one of the many free classes listed in the community events calendar. The reception room also doubles as the waiting room for the health clinic, founded in 1925 by Dr. Abraham Goodwin and his wife, Angelina Goodwin, R.N.

The health clinic is open five days a week and evenings until 8 pm. It is closed on Tuesdays and Sundays. Mrs. Goodwin explained. "We modified our office hours to accommodate the many working parents in the neighborhood. Early on, we discovered that many mothers were reluctant to come to the clinic without their husbands. Because of this, we scheduled in a longer lunch break and extended our clinic hours into evening. In addition, we offer medical care on Saturdays. We reserve Tuesdays for home visits."

Dr. Goodwin added, "So many of the immigrants are afraid to come down to the clinic. We feel it is an important service to visit them in their homes when they are ill."

The initial objective of the settlement house project was to offer healthcare to the immigrant population in Williamsburg. However once the health clinic was underway, the doctor and his wife studied the broader needs of the community to determine educational programs. "We continue to hold monthly meetings with our neighbors to identify their interests and needs. We started slowly, garnering support and volunteers for daycare for sick children recovering from long-term illnesses, such as polio." With the help of a staff of volunteers, the settlement house now provides transportation, lunch, nutritious snacks and various activities during the day to children who would otherwise be recovering at home unsupervised while their parents work.

"This year's educational offerings are designed from the community input we received at the monthly neighborhood meetings. With the assistance of community volunteers, adult English and citizenship classes are now being offered, in addition to new mother and hygiene classes." All classes are supervised by Mrs. Adeline Ferme' Steingold, R.N.

"Many immigrant mothers were having difficulty with the English language and were disappointed that they could not help their children with their homework. Working parents were concerned that their children were home alone after school with no parks or playgrounds in the neighborhood to keep them safe and active," Mrs. Goodwin said.

Nativity Settlement House is proud of their newest addition, the two-story afterschool center and backyard play structure which is a cooperative *neighborhood effort that came to fruition with financial backing from Nativity Church, the Diocese of Brooklyn and the Steingold Foundation.*

School children arrive after their school day to play, eat, rest and work on their homework assignments. After an hour of play in the backyard, they are provided with a nutritious snack and a half-hour of rest and reading. The next hour is devoted to their homework assignments and supervised by volunteer tutors. "After a busy day at school, we didn't want to overload the children immediately with schoolwork. We alternate an hour of games and active play with rest before we assist them with their homework."

When their parents come to pick them up, the children's assignments are completed, their bellies are full and their school struggles are identified. A number of volunteers work tirelessly to sustain the afterschool program. Visiting Nurse Maureen O'Shaughnessy and prospective teacher and volunteer, Leonora Bartoli, lead the volunteers in their efforts. They have put together an exciting summer enrichment program for the children in the neighborhood. Miss O'Shaughnessy said, "Many high school and college students have already signed up to volunteer to work with the children this summer."

"What's planned for the future?" this reporter asked.

The Goodwins are planning to build a summer garden with picnic tables around the new play structure. Mrs. Goodwin said, "Although the clinic is closed on Sundays, the playground and garden area will always be accessible for families to come and relax on weekends and have a picnic lunch."

Dr. Goodwin had one last message for his Williamsburg neighbors. "Don't wait until you are ill to come in to see us. Bring your children into the clinic regularly when they are well. In that way, we will have an opportunity to keep everyone in the neighborhood well and healthy. This house is your house."

"Adeline, how many times have you read that article in today's paper?" Harry asked as he walked into their bedroom to find Adeline reading *The Brooklyn Bugle*.

Adeline neatly folded the newspaper and put it down on her bed. "I think it's a wonderful article, don't you?"

"I do. It's just what you wanted, isn't it?"

"Yes, thank you for arranging it. It does make me feel better that Angie and Abe are getting the recognition they deserve. They must never know it was our idea. Promise me that you will never tell them."

"I promise."

"I was going to cut out the article and save it in my keepsake box."

"What's in that pretty box of yours?"

"Lots of things…photos of us, letters you've written to me, notes I took during the war, letters from the *tommies*. I was just reading this letter."

"Who's it from?"

"It's a letter from a nurse I met in France when we were both recuperating at the Chateau Villa Tino, the hospital for nurses in Paris Plage. Her name is Helen and we still write to each other. During the war, she was assigned to a tent hospital close to the front. The nurses at that location had a rough time of it."

"In what way?" Harry asked.

"The medical staff stationed at the tent hospital in Rouen often found that they were in the middle of the fighting. I can read her letter to you if you're interested."

"I am," Harry said as he sat down on the bed. "Go ahead."

"Right now?" Adeline asked.

"Yes, now, I love to listen to you read."

Adeline sat down on the bed next to her husband, unfolded the letter and began to read.

Chapter Sixteen

June 1918
Chateau Villa Tino
Paris Plague, France

The hands of angels work agile and quick
To change a bandage and comfort the sick.

Dearest Addie,

How is my dear hospital roommate and how are things at Le Treport hospital? I hope it's not as chaotic there as it has been in Rouen these past months. I am so sorry I haven't written like I promised when we were bedded down with trench fever at the hospital for nurses at the Chateau Villa Tino. So much has happened this spring and there was so little time to write. I am just now getting caught up on my letters and my journal writing. That is because I ended up back at the Chateau Villa Tino once again. Yes, I have been bedded down here for three whole weeks. This time I was admitted with diphtheria but I am happy to report that I am on the road to recovery and will be leaving next week to finally return to work.

After I was discharged from the hospital, I returned to Rouen to discover I was desperately needed. The hospital was filled to capacity and still the soldiers kept coming. We ran out of tents and beds and were forced to put our patients on the ground outside. The soldiers were coming directly from the front. It seems that the great spring offensive turned defensive as the Huns advanced faster than anyone thought was humanly possible. The

Jerries *bombed everything, even the* Dressing Station *near the front and the* Casualty Clearing Station, *which was only five miles away from our hospital. At the time of the invasion, the station was caring for more than seven hundred troops. All the ambulatory patients were suddenly forced up, out and onto the road. With so little time, the medics cleared out the station as best they could. They managed to get most of the soldiers to us by horse, pony-cart and on foot. Thirteen soldiers blinded by mustard-gas arrived with bandages over their eyes, after having walked all five miles hand-to-shoulder in a line with one medic leading them to safety. What a sight they were!*

When the medics returned to the Casualty Clearing Station *for the soldiers they weren't able to move out, they discovered that the* Huns *had destroyed the entire station and had shot the soldiers who were bedridden, rather than care for them. What a cruel and inhuman thing to do to the wounded. I believe that they will be punished for such a horrid war crime, either in this life or the next.*

I had no sooner arrived back at the Rouen hospital when I was put to work. Sister assigned Ruth Allen and me to the dressing tent, thinking it would be light work for us. Hour after hour and all through the day and night, the wounded soldiers from the Casualty Clearing Station *poured in. We had a system, of course. Ruth Allen was stationed at table one, ripping and pulling off bandages. After a fair share of cursing and howling, the soldiers moved on to the M.O.'s desk for their wound assessment. Then they proceeded to come to my table where I bandaged them up as quickly as I possibly could, according to the M.O.'s directives. The three of us worked over twenty-four hours straight in this manner. By the next day, we counted our logs and noted that we had dressed over five hundred wounded soldiers. Can you imagine? When I finally had time to rest and close my eyes, I continued to unroll, cut and tape bandages while I slept.*

Throughout the entire spring, the military advance has been touch and go. One day, we would receive reports that the tommies *had advanced a mile. The next day it was reported that they lost their ground and retreated a mile. This happened over and over again. We never knew if we were staying or leaving camp. There were air raids almost every night. We were ordered to head for the trenches in the hills when the air raid siren sounded. Oh the agony of leaving my warm bed in my cozy, little tent to share a dirty, wet trench with little animal friends and trying to sleep to the sound of artillery fire ringing in my ears all through the night.*

When they sent me to the hospital for nurses, I was so sick. I couldn't believe I had to leave. I tried to hide my cough and swollen glands for days. I had a sore throat which prevented me from eating or drinking. I developed a throat abscess as big as a plum. Of course, I never saw the actual size of the abscess but that's what the M.O. reported while he was draining it. I only saw the blood and pus pouring out of my mouth. It's no wonder that I couldn't breathe.

I have just received a letter from my supervisor in Rouen with April's hospital report. It states: "We hold a record for British hospitals on the Western front. In ten days, we have admitted four thousand, eight hundred and fifty-three wounded, sent four thousand to Blighty, have done nine hundred and thirty-five operations - and only twelve patients have died." The news I received from Rouen is that there is talk that my entire hospital may be dismantled and will move soon because it is too close to the fighting. Each day continues to be uncertain. I am not sure where I will end up when I return to work duty - if I will return to the hospital in Rouen or if I will be reassigned to a different station.

Dear friend, no matter what, I promise to write again when I am settled. Stay well and safe so that we don't meet up again at the Chateau.
I remain your friend,
Helen Dore Boylston (3)

Chapter Seventeen

❧

May 1926
Nativity Settlement House
Williamsburg, Brooklyn

The angels stay focused and directed,
Always prepared for the unexpected.

When Leonora Bartoli arrived at Nativity House and opened the Bartoli shoebox to show Maureen the shoes her father had made for Mrs. Tagliano, Maureen was so delighted that she cried.

Angie and Adeline came in from the reception room.

"Do let us see, dear."

Leonora proudly displayed the new shoes for everyone to admire. The tan colored shoes were made of two types of leather, a firm piece of leather for support where support was needed and a softer, more subtle section of leather where stretch was required to accommodate Mrs. Tagliano's large bunions.

"Look what he did here," Leonora said as she pointed out the workmanship on the side of each shoe. "Here he made the tiniest slits for extra stretch and lined the area with butter-soft leather."

"They're exquisite!" Adeline said.

"They're perfect! It must have taken him hours to make that design," Maureen said.

"Yes, he devoted a whole week to the project, but he will never admit to it. That's the way he is. He made me promise to throw away the shoebox and deliver them in a brown paper bag."

"No?"

"Yes, he doesn't want anyone to know he made the shoes at no cost."

"Well, shoebox or not, Mrs. Tagliano is going to absolutely love them," Maureen said looking through her daily roster of home visits. "I have her on my list for a home visit this afternoon. I'm going to go right after lunch. I can't wait to show her the shoes."

"I would love to see her face when she puts them on, Maureen."

"I'm certain she will be delighted when she sees her new shoes. Leonora, please thank your father for all of us at Nativity House." Angie added, "I'll post a thank-you note to him in today's mail."

"I will, most definitely, Nurse Angie."

"I can't wait to show them to Mrs. Tagliano," Maureen said, as she gathered up the shoes and her patients' charts, preparing to begin her first home visit of the day.

After lunch, Maureen O'Shaughnessy was so eager to reach Meserole Street that she almost skipped down the street. She couldn't wait to show Mrs. Tagliano the new shoes made specifically for her feet. Maureen knew the shoes would fit perfectly. Weeks before, Leonora had accompanied her on a home visit where she made an outline of the woman's feet on brown paper and precisely measured her feet the exact way her father had instructed her to.

Maureen found the apartment landlady, Mrs. Borkowski, sitting on the top step of the stoop in front of the apartment building.

"Good Morning, Mrs. Borkowski. How are you on this lovely day?"

"Fine, fine, sweetie, I'm just wanting to catch a bit of sunshine before it gets too hot today."

"Guess what? I have new shoes for Mrs.Tagliano."

"No fooling?"

"Do you want to let me into her apartment?"

"Maybe you can save Rosie a few steps. Why don't you try knocking on Carmela's door? I'm certain she'll open it now that she knows you."

Maureen could plainly see that Mrs. Borkowski was not about to budge from her sunny spot on the front stoop. She decided to indulge the landlady, although she knew Mrs. Tagliano was not going to answer the door.

"I'll give it a try but I'll be back if she doesn't open the door to me," the nurse said.

"Okay, sweetie, tell me your name again, dear."

"Miss O'Shaughnessy."

"Yes, Miss, if she doesn't open her door for you, come back down for me."

When Maureen knocked on the apartment door, she received no answer which was the response she expected. After walking up a flight of stairs, Maureen had to walk back down to ask Mrs. Borkowski for her assistance. As she followed the landlady up the flight of stairs once again, instead of complaining, Maureen cheerfully commented, "I certainly get lots of exercise being a visiting nurse."

Mrs. Borkowski knocked on the apartment door. "It's me, Carmela. It's Rosie. Don't be scared now. I'm coming in."

The landlady unlocked the door. They called out Carmela's name but received no reply. They searched through the apartment, going from room to room.

Finally, they found Carmela Tagliano sound asleep on the toilet in the bathroom. Mrs. Borkowski put her hand on Carmela's shoulder and gently shook her. "Wake up, Carmela. The nice nurse is here to see you again and has a surprise for you."

It took a little while before Mrs. Tagliano woke up. When she did, she looked at them, trying to decide who they were.

"Sorry to wake you, Carmela."

"Oh, I wasn't sleeping."

"What were you doing?" Mrs. Borkowski asked.

"Just resting, Rosie."

"Come. Let us help you to the kitchen."

The three women sat down at the kitchen table. "I have a gift for you, Mrs. Tagliano," Maureen said eagerly as she lifted the leather shoes out of the paper bag. "Look! I brought you new shoes. A volunteer at Nativity House made them especially for you."

Carmelo Tagliano examined the shoes. Then she said, "They look different."

"Would you like to try them on?"

"No, I don't think they will fit my feet."

"How do you know if you don't try them on?"

"I can tell, Miss. I think they will hurt."

"Please, Mrs. Tagliano, please try them on."

"No, I already know they aren't going to fit and I don't like the looks of them. They look odd."

Maureen looked to Mrs. Borkowski for help but the landlady made it clear that she did not want to get involved. "Well," said Rozalia Borkowski, "I'll be going now, dearie. I'll let you handle this."

"Mrs. Tagliano, remember when my associate came with me to your house and measured your feet for new shoes?"

"When was that?"

"It was last month."

"No, I don't remember."

"Well, she came and measured your feet so that these shoes could be made to the exact measurements of your feet."

"Really?"

"Yes, really, won't you please try them on? I will help you."

"Well, if you insist, nurse."

Maureen knelt down, took off the woman's slippers. She fitted one shoe on Mrs. Tagliano's right foot.

"Ouch!" Carmela cried out.

"I am sorry if I hurt you, Mrs. Tagliano. How do they feel?" Maureen asked, as she tied up the shoelaces.

"Ouch, my bunions!"

Maureen adjusted the shoelaces. "Perhaps they feel tight because they are new. Maybe if you walk around a bit," she suggested.

Carmela Tagliano gave Maureen a shrug but complied.

Maureen assisted Carmela as she took a few steps around the room.

"You can take them back now, Miss."

"No, I was hoping you would keep them."

"I will have to ask my daughter."

"Mrs. Tagliano, perhaps now that you have new shoes that fit you, you might like to take a walk outside?"

"I don't think so."

"What do you think about this idea? Let's take a walk around the block and if you still don't like the shoes after the walk, you won't have to wear them anymore today. How's that?"

"Okay, after that, I can take them off?"

"Yes, I promise."

Maureen helped the woman on with her light spring coat and assisted her down the stairs. Once outside, they found Rozalia Borkowski still sitting in her sunny spot.

"Ah, Carmela, I like your new shoes," Rozalia said as they passed her.

"Thank you, Rosie. You really like them?"

"Yes, I do! I certainly do!"

Maureen took Carmela's arm as they walked around the block. The first person they met as they turned the corner was Mrs. DeSouza, the florist's wife, standing in front of the store. "Good to see you out and about, Mrs. Tagliano. What fancy shoes you have on today."

"Thank you, Elsie. Do you like them?"

"Yes, I do, Carmela."

Next, they met Mario, the fruit and vegetable man. "My, my, my, Mrs. Tagliano. Nice to see you. Are those new shoes you're wearing today?"

"They certainly are, Mister Mario. Do you like them?"

"Yes, I do. Wear them in good health."

As they walked around the block, Carmela received more attention and many more compliments for her new shoes. When they returned to the apartment building, Maureen asked, "What do you think, Mrs. Tagliano? Do you like the shoes?"

"Everyone seems to like them so I guess I do, too, but I have no money to pay for them."

"As I said, a volunteer made them as a gift for you."

"What do I have to do in return?"

"Nothing, Mrs. Tagliano, simply enjoy them."

"You get nothing for nothing, you know."

"There is no catch today and no payment is necessary."

"Well then, nurse, as a favor to you, I think I will keep these funny looking shoes and try to get used to them."

Maureen was in the hallway, helping Carmela Tagliano up the flight of stairs when the building shook and they heard a crashing thump overhead.

"What's that?" Carmela asked.

"I don't know. It sounded like it came from upstairs," Maureen answered.

Mr. and Mrs. Borkowski came running out of their ground floor apartment.

"What's all the racket?" Mr. Borkowski yelled.

"Did the old lady fall?" Mrs. Borkowski asked.

"No, it came from up there," Maureen pointed to the roof. "It sounded like the roof caved in."

"I better go check. Stay here, ladies. I'll let you know if it's safe to go up." Mr. Borkowski rushed up the stairs taking two steps at a time, passing the women on the way. The landlady and the nurse helped Carmela down to the first floor landing and waited for Mr. Borkowski to report on his findings. When he reached the third floor landing, he stopped and listened. He heard crying coming from one of the apartments.

"It's the girls," he called out, pulling the apartment key from the key ring that was attached to his belt.

"What's going on in there?" he asked. "What are you girls up to?"

A tiny little voice answered. "Nothing, Mr. Borkowski."

"I'm coming in."

Gleason Borkowski opened the door and found the apartment covered in a white fog. As he waded through chunks of plaster on the floor, he realized that the plaster ceiling had fallen. He found the two little girls huddled in a corner on the other side of the room covered in a layer of white.

"What happened here?" he asked.

"We don't know," little Hildie said.

Her older sister, Hanna, added, "We didn't do it!"

Chapter Eighteen

The Same Day
Nativity Settlement House
Williamsburg, Brooklyn

When angels try to do their best,
They sometimes will be put to test.

As Nurse Angie Goodwin was checking her supplies in the kitchen utility room at Nativity House, Maureen walked through the front door with two frightened little girls who were clinging to her and crying their eyes out.

"What happened? Why are they covered in flour?"

"It's plaster. Did Doctor Abe leave for his house calls? Is he still here?"

"Yes, he's here. He came back to the clinic after lunch. He's inside. Come." Angie motioned for Maureen to follow her into the examination room area where they found Dr. Abe Goodwin.

"What happened?" he asked.

"We didn't do nothin'. We were just playing with our cutouts," Hanna mumbled and coughed.

"The ceiling in their apartment fell," Maureen explained.

"Was anyone else hurt?" Doctor Abe asked.

"No, they were home alone."

"...and the whole ceiling fell on them?"

Maureen answered, "Apparently a section of the plaster ceiling in the corner of the living room fell, but it was enough to frighten the girls and cover the whole apartment in white plaster. I wanted to call an ambulance but the landlord refused to let me use his telephone. He said that if I called for an ambulance, the city authorities would make a big deal of it. He wanted to keep the whole thing quiet. 'Hush hush', he said. He didn't want to call attention to the accident and said he would fix everything right away. I told him that the girls might have gotten hurt and needed to be checked out by a doctor. I told him that I was taking the girls to the settlement house clinic and he wasn't going to stop me. I took the girls and left the apartment."

"Is that the apartment building where Mrs. Tagliano lives?" Angie asked.

"Yes, I brought her the shoes today," Maureen explained. "We took a short walk around the block and then this happened. The girls were home alone."

"Where's their mother?" Angie asked.

"Their mother works. The older one should be in school but the mother didn't enroll her. The landlady said their mother didn't want the little one left alone all day."

"Where is the father?" Abe asked as he began checking for injuries and broken bones.

"I don't know. I don't follow the family. They were never referred to me. There's no case file."

"My Papa's in the army," Hildie said, interrupting them.

"He is not, Hildie! Stop telling that story." Hanna coughed. "It's not true."

"Maybe it is," Hildie insisted, "or maybe he got sick and is in the hospital."

Hanna looked up at the doctor and coughed again. "Don't mind her. She likes to tell stories that aren't true."

Angie heard a knock on the front door. She went to open the door but Mrs. Borkowski had let herself in and walked right into the examination area while Dr. Abe was conducting his assessment.

"Does anything hurt?" he asked.

Both girls shook their head and answered, "No."

Rozalia Borkowski asked, "How are the girls?"

"I can't stop coughing, Mrs. Borkowski."

"Are you their mother?" Dr. Abe asked.

"No, I'm the landlady. My husband sent me down to see if they are all right. He is very concerned."

"He didn't appear very concerned a few minutes ago," Maureen replied. "He wouldn't let me call an ambulance."

"He was upset and wasn't thinking clearly. He sent me down to see if they are okay."

"He said he didn't want any trouble with the city," Maureen said.

"He did nothing wrong. The ceilings in these old buildings crumble and fall all the time."

"You mean this has happened before?" Angie asked.

"Please don't get the wrong idea. My husband is a good landlord. Why, he's cleaning up the mess right now. He'll get it fixed as soon as possible. I'll take the girls home now," Mrs. Borkowski said, reaching for Hildie's hand. "Come, Hildie."

Dr. Abe disagreed, "No, I prefer to have them stay here a while so I can observe them."

"What do I tell their mother when she comes home and her girls aren't home?"

"Tell her that she can pick up her girls right here at Nativity House."

"I don't think she will appreciate that."

"What are their names?" Angie asked.

"Hanna and Hilda Tatjana."

"…And their mother?"

"Vilhelmina Tatjana."

"…And their father?"

"I don't know. I think he ran off on Vilhelmina a long time ago."

"Please tell Mrs. Tatjana that the girls are here."

"She's working. She won't be home until six."

"That's fine. That will give us time to observe the girls for any unfavorable effects."

Mrs. Borkowski insisted, "I really think I should take the girls home."

"You are welcome to stay here and keep the girls company," Angie said.

"I don't have time. I have to help my husband."

Angie was firm. "As I said, we will watch over them until their mother comes to pick them up this evening."

"Okay," Mrs. Borkowski said, "…but I don't think that's right. I think I should take the girls home now." She left in a huff and slammed the door behind her.

At 6:20, Vilhelmina Tatjana rang the bell at Nativity House.

After she introduced herself, Dr. Abe explained his findings to Vilhelmina and instructed her on what to observe during the night.

"If they complain of pain, appear disoriented…," he began.

"I have to go to work tonight."

"Surely, you aren't thinking of leaving them home alone tonight?" Dr. Abe questioned.

"Mrs. Tatjana, I'm afraid we can't release the children to your care, if you can't stay with them," Angie explained.

"My landlady might be able to watch them."

"I don't think that's a good idea."

"I suppose I can call my boss and tell him that the girls are sick, but I may lose my job."

"Where do you work in the evening?"

"I got a job checking hats at the Roseland Ballroom. Since my husband left, I've been working two jobs."

"…And you leave the girls home alone every night?"

"They aren't alone. They are good girls. They watch each other. It won't be forever, you know. I'm also taking a night class once a week to learn shorthand. I'm learning to be a private secretary."

"Where do the girls go to school?" Angie asked.

"They don't yet. They're still young. I was planning on enrolling them in September."

"It's important that you do. Hanna is old enough to be in school."

"Well, it's almost summertime."

"Mrs. Tatjana, I understand it's difficult to juggle work and the children but the children shouldn't stay home alone all day and evening. We have an exciting summer program planned for the neighborhood children. Would you like to enroll them in our summer school program?"

"When does it start, nurse?"

"At the end of June…"

"How much does it cost?"

"It's free for the children in the neighborhood."

"I don't know. I will have to think about it."

Chapter Nineteen

June 1926
New York City

From the first, the attraction was so strong,
He stood captivated by love's sweet song.

Alfonso Ferrara had been in love with Leonora Bartoli for as long as he could remember. He could trace his feelings all the way back to the first moment he spotted her as she prepared to go to Sunday Mass with her parents. He was ten years old at the time.

Alfonso had accompanied his father, Aldo Ferrara, to his shoe repair shop on Third Avenue. Aldo had asked his son to come with him that day because there were a number of shoe repair orders that needed to be filled before Monday morning. Alfonso jumped at the chance to spend time with his father at the shoe repair shop. His father worked behind a long wooden counter, which was to the right of the shoe store entrance. On the left wall were four stalls. These stalls were for customers to wait while their shoes were being repaired and polished. Each stall had a three-foot high gate, a bench and a small leather footstool. Customers came in, sat down in the stall, took off their shoes and handed them to Aldo who picked up the shoes at the stall. As soon as Aldo finished the repair, he returned the shoes to the customer who was waiting in the stall. In this way, socks were never dirtied and bare feet never touched the ground.

That Sunday morning Alfonso spent time amusing himself by going from stall to stall, in and out of each one, deciding which one he liked the best. He had a favorite one, the stall nearest the window. There he would sit for hours, sometimes pretending he was in jail and sometimes pretending he was on the witness stand at a courthouse. He watched his father work behind his cobbler's bench, soothed by the hum of the sewing machine and the familiar smell of leather and glue.

Other times, he passed the time by studying the people walking up and down Third Avenue. From the store window Alfonso watched as a little girl came out of her apartment building holding her mother's hand as her father held the door open for them. Dressed in a pale blue silk dress and straw hat with a matching blue ribbon, he thought the girl was prettier than any girl he had ever seen. His eyes eagerly followed the girl as she walked up the block with her long, dark-brown ringlets bouncing up and down with each step she took. He continued to watch her until the family turned the corner and disappeared on their way to the Catholic Church two blocks away. He knew they were a rich family. No one downtown where he lived wore clothes like that.

His father caught Alfonso watching them.

"That's-a Eugenio Bartoli," he mumbled. "He makes-a the shoes."

Alfonso had heard his father talk of Eugenio Bartoli, the shoemaker, whose handcrafted shoes were the talk of the town. Mr. Bartoli's shoe store was located directly across the street from Aldo's shoe repair shop. Alfonso knew the two men lived by the standards in the old country. His father, the common shoe repairman, would always be a step below the craftsman, the shoemaker. It did not matter whether they were in America or in the old country.

As years went by and Alfonso watched Leonora grow into a beautiful young woman, he kept his feelings to himself. No one knew of his attraction for Leonora, although his father suspected as much. Whenever he caught his son hopelessly waiting for a glimpse of the young lady, Aldo shook his head and looked up toward the heavens, knowing the infatuation that his son possessed would eventually end in disappointment. Aldo felt there was no hope for a romance between the two young people. Alfonso thought differently. Year after year, Alfonso maintained a stubborn hope while he continued to pray for a plan to make his dream a reality.

Education was the key to changing one's status in America. Alfonso knew that education was accessible to any young person willing to study and work hard. When Alfonso wasn't pining away for Leonora, he spent his time studying. Because of this, he maintained excellent grades in all his elementary and high school classes. His high grades made him eligible for City College, which he attended immediately after his high school graduation. Although Alfonso's father truly wished that his son would apprentice with him in the repair shop, he also appreciated and respected his son for his eagerness to gain an education and become a professional. After all, this was the very reason Aldo had come to America. He knew immigrating to America made it possible for his children to get ahead. Aldo was proud of his son for taking advantage of the opportunities the new country had to offer. Because of this, he did not interfere with his son's studies and accepted the fact that his son would be available to assist him in the shop only after he completed his school assignments.

When Alfonso graduated from City College, he was nominated for a scholarship offered to eligible Catholic students. It was only after he had received the award for a full scholarship to St. John's School of Law that he gained the confidence to put his plan in action and approach Leonora. Alfonso observed that in the late afternoon on Tuesdays, Wednesdays and Thursdays, Leonora would walk south along Third Avenue coming from Sixty-Fifth Street. On those days, she would appear between four-thirty and five o'clock. Alfonso made it his business to stand in the doorway of his father's repair shop at that time to catch a glimpse of Leonora as she headed home.

One day when she glanced his way, he conjured up enough courage to nod. Leonora acknowledged him with a smile. On another day she waved. Alfonso returned the wave. Soon it became their practice to greet each other from a distance on Tuesday, Wednesday and Thursday afternoons.

On one very cold afternoon in January, the temperature suddenly dropped. The puddles left by an earlier rainstorm turned into sheets of slick black ice. As Leonora stepped down from the sidewalk curb onto the street, a gust of wind whipped across the avenue, causing her to slip and fall on the ice. Alfonso lost no time in running across the street to come to her rescue. When he offered his arm to help her up, he slipped and fell beside her. As the El train roared above them, they both broke out into gales of laughter.

Alfonso was the first to stand. He assisted Leonora to her feet and introduced himself.

"Good Afternoon. I'm Alfonso Ferrara."

"Yes, I know. I've often seen you at Mr. Ferrara's shop. I know you are his son."

"...And you are Mr. Bartoli's daughter."

"Yes, my name is Leonora. Nice to meet you, Mr. Ferrara."

"The pleasure is all mine. Please call me Alfonso."

"We've seen each other a number of times. Why is it that we've never introduced ourselves before today?"

"Perhaps we were waiting for fate to introduce us. May I offer you my arm and see you to your door?"

"Why certainly, Alfonso. That's very kind of you."

"Are you coming home from work at this hour?"

"Yes, I volunteer at a settlement house in Brooklyn. Do you work at your father's shop?"

"I work afternoons and weekends. I am a student at St. Johns Law School during the day."

"You are studying to be an attorney?

"Yes, I am."

"I want to be a teacher. I am working at the settlement house to gain teaching experience. I convinced my father to allow me to attend Hunter College. He agreed to send me to college next year because I am doing so well at the settlement house."

"I'm impressed, Leonora. So you are coming from the Sixty-Seventh Street train station?"

"Yes."

"May I be so bold as to ask if I can meet you there tomorrow afternoon? They are predicting snow tomorrow and I should not like you to slip and fall again."

"Nor you," Leonora added with a smile.

"I would like to escort you home, Leonora."

"Indeed, Alfonso, I would like that very much."

After that Leonora could count on Alfonso meeting her at the El train station on Sixty-Seventh Street and Third Avenue to walk her home. Soon Alfonso and Leonora were secretly meeting in Central Park where they spent hours strolling along the park's many paths. In the summer they took the El train to Coney Island a number of times. Leonora invited her younger cousin to come along, telling her parents that she was taking her cousin to Luna Park but forgetting to mention that Alfonso would be accompanying them.

When Alfonso confessed that he was in love with Leonora, she said she felt the same.

"Let's get married," he proposed.

She knew her father would not approve of their marriage until after Alfonso finished law school.

He made a vow to her that on the day he graduated from St. John's School of Law in June of 1927, he would go to see her father and ask for her hand in marriage.

Their clandestine courtship progressed in this fashion for a year until the day that Leonora promised her father she would meet Fulgenzio Rossi, the son of her father's paisan, Fosco Rossi, a friend from the old country and the owner of a very popular Italian restaurant in the city. Alfonso was heartbroken when Leonora told him. He begged her to not go with Fulgenzio. He reassured her that he would graduate law school the following year and was worthy enough to approach her father to ask for her hand in marriage.

"How can you do this to me, Leonora?" he asked.

"I am only going out to dinner with him at his family's Italian restaurant. My father and mother will be there."

"You must tell your father about me."

"I can't, not right now. It is too soon. You haven't graduated. We agreed to wait."

"Please, Leonora, I can't bear the thought of you spending even a minute with Fat Fulgenzio."

"Understand, Alfonso, it will only be this one time. I assure you and it's rude to call him *fat*."

"Well he is. One meeting may lead to two. I can't even imagine such a thing. I love you, Leonora. You are breaking my heart."

"I love you, Alfonso. Please understand."

"I do not understand. I think you may be ashamed of me. I will be taking my leave now. Goodbye, Leonora." Alfonso turned and left, leaving Leonora standing on her doorstep.

"Alfonso, wait! Don't go."

Alfonso was angry. His father had been right all along. Alfonso would never measure up in the eyes of the Bartolis no matter how many educational degrees he had under his belt. Clearly, Mr. Bartoli had plans for his daughter which did not include him.

Chapter Twenty

June 1926
Williamsburg, Brooklyn

With so many things to do today,
She's planning for her wedding day.

It was the second week of June. Spring was in the air and summer was around the corner. Maureen O'Shaughnessy's thoughts constantly drifted to her upcoming wedding to Sam Goodwin in September. She had less than four months to complete preparations for the big day. Luckily at her mother's insistence, she had scheduled an appointment at Madame Renee's Bridal Boutique during the month of March. Together they had spent an afternoon at the store and selected a wedding gown that everyone agreed was perfect for Maureen's petite figure. She loved the gorgeous bridal gown and pearl headdress she had chosen. The fashionable mid-calf length and scalloped hem of the gown made her appear taller than her five feet, and the fullness of the lace skirt filled out her slim figure. Earlier in the week, Madame Renee left a message that the bridal gown would soon be ready for fittings.

As she traveled to and from work, Maureen made mental notes of the many things that were left to do. When she arrived at her destination, she wrote them down. The list grew longer and longer each day. The flower girl's and bridesmaids' dresses hadn't been selected yet. It was getting increasingly difficult for everyone to agree on a time when they could all go to the bridal shop together. She had asked Adeline's daughter, Sadie, to be her flower girl but Sadie wasn't available to select her dress until after school let out for the summer.

Maureen had disagreed with her mother about the color of the bridesmaids' dresses. Maureen envisioned a bridal party dressed in autumn gold and orange to match the colors of the fall flowers. Her mother had objected, saying such harsh colors were inappropriate for a church wedding. It was Leonora, her maid of honor, who saved the day. When Leonora proposed a pale peach color that would blend in with the autumn bouquets, her mother approved and so did Maureen.

Maureen was now confident that all the bouquets and flower arrangements would be prepared to her satisfaction. She had panicked when Sam first approached her with the idea of using the family's long-term funeral florist for their wedding flowers. She pictured masses of white wreaths in the shape of sympathy crosses draped down the church pews until Sam assured Maureen of Mr. Fazio's many talents. It took only one meeting with Mr. Fazio to convince Maureen that his skill in floral design was not limited to funerals.

There were also the meetings with Father Salvia which had to be scheduled. The couple was required to meet with the priest before the bands of marriage could be posted.

A passing streetcar brought Maureen back to the reality of the workday and her prescheduled home visits. There were a number of patients to visit on her calendar. Her last stop of the day would be at the Borkowskis' apartment building. There she planned to have a conversation with Mrs. Moratelli and, hopefully, Mrs. Tatjana after the women came home from work. Marghereta Moratelli had signed her boys up for summer school at the settlement house but hadn't enrolled her mother in the eldercare program. In addition, Maureen wanted to ask Mrs. Moratelli if she would help her convince Vilhemina Tatjana to enroll her little girls, Hilda and Hanna, in the summer enrichment program. Maureen hated the thought of the girls being home alone all summer.

Heaven only knows what trouble they could get into this summer especially if the landlady is the only one keeping an eye on them throughout the day.

Maureen waited until after six in the evening to ring Mrs. Moratelli's apartment doorbell. Marghereta Moratelli answered without delay.

"Who's there?" she asked.

"Mrs. Moratelli, I'm Visiting Nurse O'Shaughnessy. We haven't met but I am the visiting nurse who has been coming every week to check on your mother."

"What can I do for you?"

"I'd like to check your mother's feet this evening."

Marghereta opened the door.

"Come in. Isn't it a little late for you to be making a home visit?" Marghereta asked as she escorted Maureen into the kitchen. She walked to the kitchen table where her boys were finishing their dinner. "Would you like to sit down, nurse? Boys, this is Nurse O'Shaughnessy. She's from the settlement house and has come to see Nana. Say hello to her."

"Hi, Nurse!" Mikey said, continuing to eat.

"Hello," mumbled Johnny.

"I know it's late and I'm sorry to be interrupting your dinner. I had a number of home visits scheduled today. I saved your mother's visit for last so that I could introduce myself to you."

"Would you care to join us for supper? I have extra."

"Oh, no, thank you. I have dinner plans tonight. This is my last home visit of the day. How is your mother this evening?"

"I prepared her supper as soon as I got home from work. She gobbled it down. Now she's sound asleep on the couch."

"Has she been wearing her new shoes?"

"Yes, she has been enjoying them. She loves them. She wears them every day."

"Has she complained of her bunions hurting her?"

"No, not since she got the new shoes."

"Well, that's encouraging to hear."

"Do you want me to wake her up, nurse?"

"There's no need to disturb her if she's sleeping. I'd like to take a peek at her and check her pulse if you don't mind."

"Sure, go ahead. She's in there." Marghereta pointed to the next room.

Maureen went into the living room to check Mrs. Tagliano's feet. The elderly woman slept through the nurse's assessment.

Returning to the kitchen, Maureen said. "Mrs. Moratelli, I'd like to talk to you about signing your mother up for the eldercare program at the Settlement House this summer."

"I talked to her about that. She said she doesn't want to go."

"Do you think there is any way I could change her mind?" Maureen asked.

"I don't think so. She says she's fine staying home with the boys."

"Perhaps, but…"

"Also, you see, the boys are now having second thoughts about going to summer school." Marghereta looked over at her son, Mikey.

"I signed you up for the summer program at the Settlement House. You remember I told you."

"Yeah, but remember we told you that we didn't want to go. Heck! You can send little Johnny-boy if you want but I'm not going."

"Watch your language in front of the nurse, Michael."

"It's just that all the kids on the block will laugh at me. Nobody goes to school in the summer."

Johnny-boy put his fork down. "I'm not going if Mikey isn't going."

Maureen explained. "It's not really a school. We just call it that."

"Why?"

"I'm sure I don't know the answer to that question."

"Well, what is it then, if it's not a school?" Mikey asked.

Maureen thought for a moment. "It's more like camp!"

"Where we get to sleep outside and go on hikes?"

"Not exactly," Maureen hesitated, "but we have interesting activities planned for the boys and girls in the neighborhood."

"Girls! I've heard enough. Now I'm really not interested in going." Mikey looked over at his little brother and explained. "Johnny-boy, they'll have us doing girlie things, like art stuff and planting flowers."

"I guarantee you that you won't have to do art. We have many other projects. The boys' program could be totally different from the girls' activities."

"Like what?"

"We have Mr. Fyne scheduled to come every day. He is a retired carpenter who offered to volunteer to teach all the boys how to work with wood. The first project they will work on is making boxcar scooters."

Johnny-boy looked up at his older brother. "That doesn't sound so bad, Mikey?"

Maureen continued. "Yes, and when your boxcar is finished, you can decorate and paint it anyway you wish. We'll have a boxcar race in the schoolyard when the cars are completed."

"Will we have to act in stupid plays and stuff like that?"

"No, only those children, who are interested in acting, will select the drama activity."

"So we would get to pick?"

"Yes, of course, you choose the kind of activities you like to do."

"What else do you have?" Mikey asked.

"We received permission to have a baseball team play in the Catholic school playground across the street."

"Really?"

"Yes, you see, when you arrive you will select the type of things you want to do this summer."

"That sounds okay to me but what if we don't like it?"

"You are free to try another activity."

"If I were you boys, I'd go and give it a try. I'd see what it was like and then decide," Marghereta told her sons.

Mikey shrugged. "Okay, we'll try it. Johnny-boy and I will go."

"I'd like your grandmother to come also," Maureen added.

"What's she gonna do with all the kids playing around there?"

Maureen explained. "There is a special program for older people in a different section of the house."

Marghereta turned to Maureen. "I talked to my mother about attending but she said she wasn't interested. She said she had to watch the boys."

"The boys will be at the settlement house. She will be all alone in a hot apartment all summer. Is there any way we can talk her into coming? We have volunteer neighbors coming every day to read to the elders. They will do arts and craft projects and card games. Nutritious hot lunches will be served every day. The neighborhood ladies are volunteering their time."

"Can she see the boys? Maybe I can talk her into it if I ask her to keep an eye on the boys while they are at the settlement house."

"Would you?"

"I'll give it another try."

"Mrs. Moratelli…"

"You can call me, Greta."

"Greta, do you know Mrs. Tatjana?" Maureen asked. "She lives upstairs from you."

"Yes, we sometimes meet on the trolley on our way home from work. We walked home together from the trolley stop tonight."

"I'd like to enroll her girls in the summer program but I haven't been able to convince her. Would you come upstairs with me to talk to her?"

"I can go with you while the boys are finishing up their supper, but I can't stay long. I have to clean up."

"Thank you, I don't think it will take too long."

Marghereta gave instructions to her sons. "Boys, I'm going upstairs for a few minutes with the nurse. Finish up your dinner and don't fight while I am away. I don't want any trouble. Call me if Nona wakes up. I won't be long."

"Promise?"

"Yes, I promise."

Marghereta took off her flowered apron and opened the door for Maureen. She followed Maureen up one flight of stairs to the third floor apartment of Vilhelmina Tatjana.

Maureen knocked on the door.

There was no answer.

She knocked again.

Then Marghereta knocked. "Willie, it's me, Greta. I'm here with the nice visiting nurse from the settlement house. Are you there?" Marghereta called from the hallway.

Again, the women were met with silence.

"That's odd. I left her only a half-hour ago," Marghereta said.

"Do you think they went out?" Maureen asked.

"I don't think so, nurse. She should be home. She usually doesn't leave until seven."

"Perhaps she took the girls out for a little stroll."

"I suppose but she usually doesn't. I mean she should be cooking supper for the girls now."

She tried calling Vilhelmina a second time. "Willie, Willie..."

"Hush, listen!" Maureen whispered.

"Did you hear something, nurse?"

"I thought I did but I guess not. I suppose we should go. You have to get back to your boys. I'll try again on Thursday. Have a good evening. Thank you for your help, Greta."

"No problem. Wish I could have helped you. Good night, nurse."

Chapter Twenty-One

Later That Evening
Williamsburg, Brooklyn

You can bet, without a doubt,
Fear won't let them in or out.

"Hildie, it's time to take a bath."

"I don't wanna…"

"But Mom said…"

"I don't care. I don't wanna."

"Why?"

"The water's too cold."

Hanna couldn't argue with that. The water was too cold. Her mother had taken the bathtub down from the kitchen wall and filled it halfway with water before she left to go out. She told Hanna to give Hildie her bath and off she went to take the train into the city.

Hanna wondered: *Why couldn't she stay home like the other mothers?*

Other mothers worked but, after working all day, they came home and stayed home with their kids. They fed their children chicken soup, read bedtime stories to them, kissed them and put them to bed. No, her mother came home and went out again, all dolled up, wearing those shiny black dresses with the fringe at the bottom and her long pearl necklace with the matching earrings.

Hanna hated to be left alone to take care of Hildie. It wouldn't be so bad if Hildie did what she was told but her little sister was always giving her a hard time and not listening.

"Okay," Hanna told her sister. "I'll boil some water to make your bath warmer."

"Promise and hope to die?" Hildie asked, giving Hanna a smile.

"Yes, I cross my heart and hope to die. Look, Hildie, I'm doing it right now."

Hanna filled a small pot with water and reached for the wooden matches to light the gas burner.

"Let me light the match, Hanna."

"No, it's too dangerous."

"I can do it."

"You are too little."

"Meanie! I can do it. You know I can."

"You can't. You could burn yourself. You could end up like Felix, the boy down the street. He's still in the hospital, you know. Little children are not supposed to play with matches."

"You think you're so big."

"I am bigger than you. Please, Hildie, you must never, never touch the matches."

"Why?"

"I told you. They are very dangerous."

"Why do you get to do everything?"

"I know what I am doing."

Hildie moaned, "I know, too."

"Hildie, stop arguing with me! The rule is that you must never touch the matches," Hanna insisted.

"I never do."

"Do, too. I found you playing with them last week. They were the matches you stole from Mrs. Tagliano. Don't you remember?"

"I did not."

"Did too. You are lying."

"Am not!" Hildie insisted.

Hildie was lying. Hanna had caught her little sister with a handful of wooden matches. She was trying to light them on the brickwork outside. Luckily, Hanna found her in time. Hildie always caused Hanna to worry. What if Hildie burned herself? What if she started a fire? Hanna heard the fire engines racing through the neighborhood with their alarms blasting day and night. Each time she heard the sirens, she froze in fright.

When Hanna asked her sister where she got the matches, Hildie told her she found them in the street. Hanna knew she was lying. The matches came from Mrs. Tagliano's apartment. Mrs. Tagliano used them to light her cigarettes but Hildie would never admit she stole them.

Hildie stole other things from Mrs. Tagliano. One several occasions Hanna found things in their apartment that belonged to Mrs. Tagliano and forced Hildie to return the stolen goods. Just because the old lady couldn't see very well, it didn't mean that Hildie could take anything she wanted. Hildie took a pen and hid it in her dress pocket. As if Hanna wasn't going to find it? Hildie was always leaving her clothes on the floor for Hanna to pick up.

Hildie even took money. Most of the time it was just a few pennies but once she took a whole dime. She asked Hanna to walk her to the store, telling her a huge lie that their mother had given her the money to buy candy and a pickle but Hanna wasn't stupid. Mother would never do that. She wouldn't give them money to buy treats. If she ever did, she wouldn't give a whole dime to Hildie. No, Hanna went right back to Mrs. Tagliano's apartment and returned the money to the old lady's pocketbook when she wasn't looking.

Hanna didn't blame Hildie. Hildie simply didn't know better. She didn't know any rules. She didn't know how to listen. They teach all that at school. Maybe if their mother had sent them to school like she was supposed to, Hildie could learn to be good.

Why won't my mother sign us up for school? Hanna wondered.

Hanna desperately wanted to go to school like the other kids. She wanted to learn to read. She wanted to read all the books in the library. Her mother said she could read the books by looking at the pictures. Hanna knew that wasn't right.

Hanna had snuck out with Hildie and gone to the library twice. Her mother never found out. Hanna could do whatever she wanted and never get caught. Hanna loved going to the library but Hildie made it difficult. She walked too slowly, always wanting to hold Hanna's hand and pretend to be a baby. At the library she talked too much no matter how many times Hanna told her little sister to be quiet. The last time they went, the librarian asked them to leave and come back with an adult. Just once, Hanna wished she could go to the library without her little sister tagging along. If she could, she would spend the whole day there, looking at all the books.

After Hanna bathed Hildie, powdered her and put on her nightgown, she lay in bed beside her until her little sister fell asleep. Hanna couldn't sleep. She got up and sat on the bedside chair in the darkness. There were so many things to worry about.

ANGELS IN BROOKLYN

She worried if the building they were living in was safe. She worried about what she would do if the house caught fire in the middle of the night while they were sleeping. She worried about not waking up in time to save both Hildie and herself from burning to death in their beds.

She worried and wondered why Mr. Borkowski never fixed the hole in the ceiling after the ceiling fell. She imagined a bad man crawling in from the roof through that hole.

She wondered if the beating sound she heard was her heartbeat coming from deep inside her or was it the sound of the footsteps of the wild gypsies coming to get her.

She wondered why she couldn't go to school like the other children.

She wondered why her father didn't come home.

She wondered why her mother pretended no one was home when the nice nurse from the settlement house knocked on the door earlier in the evening.

She thought. *Why did my mother tell me to sit still and not make a sound?*

"Shh," Mama had whispered. "Be quiet. Be very quiet."

She wondered why her mother wouldn't open the door.

Tears started to fall. Hanna wiped them away with the back of her hand.

She knelt down and said her prayers.

Dear Lord, it's me, Hanna. I know I should be thankful for my food and everything I have but I still have a lot of things to ask you. First off, I want to ask you if you could send my father back home to us. Even if he can't come home for good, maybe he could come on Hildie's birthday or maybe send her a letter on her birthday. That would make her so happy. I know if he came on my birthday, I would throw my arms around him and tell him how much I love him. Tell him

I am not asking for money or a present or anything like that. I am just asking to see him and ask him if he is okay.

Next thing I am asking is to please make my mother stay home with us when it starts to get dark. I don't understand why she has to get dressed up all the time and go out every night. The other mothers stay home and she doesn't. Another thing, can you please make her sign me up for school? I want to go so badly and I really want to go to that summer school the nurse was talking about. God, here's the last thing. Please keep Hildie safe. Please tell her to do what I ask her to do. Good night God and, one more thing, thank you for listening.

Chapter Twenty-Two

○○

July 1926
Nativity Settlement House
Williamsburg, Brooklyn

When angels perform their noble deeds,
They never show that they have needs.

When Maureen passed by Mr. Penzolli standing in front of his pork store, Mr. Penzolli tipped his hat with an evening greeting.

"Evening, nurse. How ya doin'? Hot enough for you today?"

"Yes, it is. How are you, Mr. Penzolli? I thought by this time of day, it would start to cool down but it feels hotter than ever."

"So hot you can fry an egg on the sidewalk."

Maureen felt the hot concrete through the soles of her shoes. She giggled when she mentally pictured someone trying to actually cook an egg outside on the cement.

"Can I get you anything this evening?" Mr. Penzolli asked.

"No, thank you. It's too hot to cook. I think I'll just have a salad for supper."

"I suppose everyone is thinking along those lines. My shop hasn't seen a customer since three o'clock."

Although it was past dinnertime, Maureen wasn't hungry. She was tired and thirsty. She had spent the better part of the afternoon checking on the elderly, putting wet washcloths on their foreheads and making sure she left them with enough water to drink. She knew the elderly were especially susceptible to the heat. Maureen felt the perspiration dripping down the back of her neck and longed to get out of her visiting nurse uniform. She couldn't wait to go to Nativity House to sit in the cool back office to write up her nursing notes before Sam came to drive her home.

When she arrived at Nativity House, all was quiet. There were no clinics scheduled on Tuesday evenings and the summer school children had gone home. Maureen heard hushed whispers coming from the front of the house.

She followed the sounds into the kitchen. There she found Nurse Angie and Leonora sitting at the table, sipping tall glasses of lemon iced tea. They appeared to be having a private conversation.

"Hi, I'm sorry. I heard someone talking. I wondered who was here. It wasn't my intention to disturb you," Maureen said.

"Hi, Maureen, you look a sight! Your cheeks are flushed."

"I'm okay but I am hot and tired. I did some extra visits this afternoon to check on the elderly on my roster."

"Abe was also worried about them. He went out earlier today and is still out. Meanwhile, I went into the city to meet my sister."

"How is Celestina? Will she be working here again this summer?"

"No, as a senior nursing student she's only allowed two weeks off."

"She's a senior already?"

"Yes, she will be a senior nurse in September. She'll be graduating from Bellevue School of Nursing next year. Our friend Fannie is also graduating. She worked as a nursing assistant with Adeline and me. Celestina and Fannie started the nursing program together. They'll both be registered nurses next June. I'm so proud of them."

Maureen asked, "Do you think they would be interested in becoming visiting nurses? Henry Street Settlement House needs more nurses to do home visits."

"...Or maybe Angie will hire them to come and work here with us at Nativity House," Leonora suggested.

"Actually, today Celestina and Fannie were asking me about my nursing experiences at Ellis Island Hospital. They were talking about applying to work there when they graduate," Angie said.

"That's where Adeline worked, too, right?" Leonora asked.

"Yes. Of course it all depends on whether or not Sister Hanover has openings for new nurses next year."

"Would you like that, Angie?"

"Working at Ellis Island Hospital is hard work but it will give them good hospital experience. I'm certain they will decide what is best for them when the time comes." Angie looked at Maureen. "Maureen, your cheeks are red. Please sit down and relax. Can I get you something to drink?"

"Yes, thank you, Angie."

"Would you like a glass of iced tea?"

"Yes, please. That sounds wonderful. I am thirsty. I'd love a drink." Maureen turned to Leonora and asked, "Leonora, you usually don't stay this late into the evening. How come you're still here at Nativity House?"

"Sam came by looking for you. He told me that he was planning on driving you home into the city tonight. When he saw me talking to Angie, he ordered me to stay put and insisted that he was going to give me a ride home since it was on his way. Angie called my father and he said it was okay. Sam said he'd be back in an hour to pick us up."

Maureen nodded in agreement. "That's a wonderful idea. It's too hot tonight for you to be traveling alone on the streetcar."

"Leonora was just telling me about Alfonso," Angie said.

"Is he still mad at you?" Maureen asked.

"Yes, he won't talk to me."

"Oh, I am sorry. I suppose he's still sore about that Fulgenzio fellow. I was certain that Alfonso would have come around by now."

"I really hurt his feelings when I went out with Fulgenzio. He thinks my father will talk me into marrying Fulgenzio. He doesn't understand it was just that one time. I can't stand Fulgenzio Rossi. I did it as a favor to my father but Alfonso doesn't see it that way. He thinks I'm ashamed of him."

"Why don't you go over and talk to his father?"

"I tried. His father said he will come around. 'Give him time,' he told me but he did promise to talk to him."

"How long has it been?"

"It's been over a month. Alfonso doesn't meet me anymore. Yesterday, I saw him duck into the shoe repair shop when he saw me coming home. I don't know what to do."

"I agree with his father. I think you have to give him more time. Try to be patient. His father said he will talk to him. I'm certain that Alfonso will come around eventually. He loves you."

Leonora shrugged. "How long do you think I will have to wait?"

"Perhaps he may be waiting to see what you do, to see if you will go out with Fulgenzio again."

"I hope so because I'm never going out with that Rossi boy as long as I live. You can bet on that."

"I have an idea. What if you invited Alfonso over for dinner with your family?" Angie suggested.

"My father still doesn't know about him, Nurse Angie. That's the problem. I never told my parents that I am seeing someone. Alfonso and I agreed to wait until after he graduated from law school. When Alfonso learned that my father wanted me to date Fulgenzio, he got angry and insisted I tell my father immediately."

"You couldn't do that?" Angie asked.

"I didn't think it was the right time. I know my father. He will be furious when I tell him that I have been dating Alfonso without his knowledge. No, I think we will have to wait until after Alfonso graduates. Then I will tell him."

"That's if Alfonso ever forgives you." Maureen moaned. "This is all my fault."

Angie shook her head and asked, "Why do you say that?"

"I feel like I got Leonora into this because of Mrs. Tagliano and her new shoes." Maureen turned to Leonora and apologized. "I'm so sorry."

"It's not your fault. It was totally my idea."

"I don't mean to change the subject but how is Mrs. Tagliano, Maureen?" Angie asked. "Her grandsons have been having a ball here. I think they are really enjoying the summer program."

"I checked on Mrs. Tagliano this afternoon. It was very hot in the apartment. It's a shame she has to stay cooped up in there all day. I can't talk her into coming down. I even used her grandsons as an excuse. She said she's doing fine. Some days, I feel like a complete failure."

"Don't be so hard on yourself, Maureen. You are doing the best you can do."

"Yes, well, I couldn't convince Mrs. Tatjana to send her girls to us either."

"Did you ever get to sit down and talk to her face to face?"

"No, she won't even answer the door for me although I know she's home."

"Why is that?" Leonora asked.

"I suppose she feels that I am bothering her. She's made up her mind and doesn't want to discuss it any further with me."

"It's her right and it's not your fault."

"Do you think she will sign them up for school in September, Angie?" Maureen asked.

"I don't know. At least, the law is on your side. She will be visited by a truant officer if she doesn't."

"Would you report her?"

"Abe said he would."

"That makes me feel better. The girls will be in school in a few months' time."

"Don't worry yourself so. Let's cheer up by talking about something fun. How are your wedding dress fittings coming along?"

"Oh, I love my dress. It's so beautiful. That's all I can tell you. Wait until you see it. I've already had two fittings and the dress is almost finished. Madame Renee told me it will fit perfectly as long as I don't lose any more weight."

"After this busy summer, you just might."

"If I lose weight, Madame Renee promised to do a final fitting a week before the wedding."

"When are the bridesmaids going to get their dresses?"

"We won't be going until August. No one is available before that."

"Does that give you enough time?" Angie asked.

"Yes, Madame Renee said she would be able to sew all the dresses in time and will even have plenty of time left over to do alterations. It's all planned. Leonora and my two cousins are coming. Adeline is bringing Sadie to pick her flower girl dress. Angie, would you like to come? You're invited if you would like to join us."

"Well, I might join you if it's a quiet day here at the clinic. I'd love to go along and share in the excitement. I'm glad things are falling into place for your wedding."

"I can't wait," Leonora frowned. "Although, I guess I will be one, lonely, unescorted maid-of-honor."

"Cheer up, Leonora. I'm sure Alfonso will forgive you long before the wedding. Why, I can picture the two of you dancing at Maureen's wedding right now."

Leonora sighed, "I hope so, Angie. I really hope so."

Chapter Twenty-Three

∾

July 1926
Williamsburg, Brooklyn

A plan that doesn't go so well,
And a secret she will never tell.

The sun never came out the day Hanna Tatjana decided to sneak away to the library without her sister, Hildie. She had dreamed about her escape for days but Mrs. Borkowski kept interrupting her plan. The summer heat wave had caused the landlady to be overly concerned about the girls' welfare. On more than one occasion, Mrs. Borkowski had climbed up to their third floor apartment after lunch to check on the girls.

Hanna knew that the landlady was really checking to see if they were playing out on the fire escape. On hot days when the air in the apartment was thick and heavy, Hanna knew they could always find a little breeze out on the fire escape, especially in the afternoon when the sun moved to the front of the building and the fire escape was in the shade. On those days Hanna brought out two pillows and put down a blanket to cover the iron bars. The sisters had lunch outside, pretending they were having a picnic in a park. After Hildie ate her lunch, Hanna allowed her sister to take her afternoon nap on the fire escape.

Earlier in the week, just when Hildie had fallen asleep, Mrs. Borkowski came knocking on the door. Hanna had to quickly wake up Hildie and throw all the blankets and pillows inside before she answered the door. She knew to mess up her hair, too. Mrs. Borkowski asked her, "What took you so long to answer the doorbell, Hanna dear?"

Hanna pretended to yawn and stretch out her arms. "Sorry about that, Mrs. Borkowski. My sister and I were napping."

Then Mrs. Borkowski snooped around to see if everything was to her liking and began her lecture about not going out on the fire escape because it was much too dangerous for little girls to play out there. Hanna knew that was because Mr. Borkowski had never repaired the rusty hook that held up the ladder. She knew the fire escape ladder was not supposed to touch the sidewalk.

Hanna politely smiled back at the landlady. "We would never do such a thing, never," she solemnly declared.

"Unless there was a fire, of course," the landlady added.

"Of course, Mrs. Borkowski," Hanna answered.

When the landlady came up, she didn't stay very long and sometimes she brought an apple for the girls to share.

On the afternoon Hanna went to the library, she looked out the window and saw that the day was overcast. She knew the cooler weather would prevent Mrs. Borkowski from coming up and checking on them. There was no sign of the landlady when Hanna tucked Hildie into bed for her afternoon nap. Hanna waited until she was certain her sister was fast asleep. That was one thing that she could always count on but never understood. How could little Hildie fall asleep so quickly while Hanna lay awake in bed forever or, at least, what seemed like forever?

When Hanna heard Hildie breathing heavily, she left the apartment through the fire escape. It was too risky to try to sneak through the hallway and leave the house by the front door. She would have had to slowly tiptoe down two flights of stairs, being very careful not to make the slightest sound or Mrs. Tagliano would wake up when Hanna reached the second floor. Once down in the lobby, Hanna knew that the creaking floorboards on the first floor landing could alert Mrs. Borkowski and cause her to come out into the hall to investigate.

It was faster for Hanna to use the fire escape. With the ladder touching the ground, she could easily climb down. Once she was safely down on the sidewalk, she ran all the way to the library. There she greeted the librarian with a courtesy. She wanted to show the librarian that she had arrived alone and was not in the company of her noisy little sister. Hanna quickly settled into a chair with a handful of books that caught her eye. She looked at the clock on the wall in front of her. She didn't know how to tell time but she did know that each number on the clock stood for one full hour. When she arrived at the library, the little hand had been on the one. She would have to leave when it settled on the number two.

Hanna looked through the five books she selected. When she was finished with them, she exchanged them for five more and then another five after that. She looked up at the clock. The little hand was slowly approaching the number two.

All too soon it was time to leave.

She returned the books to their proper place on the library shelf, whispered a *good-day* to the librarian and ran toward home.

As she was running, she heard the piercing shrill of the fire engine sirens behind her. She stopped long enough to make the sign of the cross. She shivered. Something deep inside her bones told her that the fire trucks were on their way to her house. When she reached the corner of her street, her worst fear was verified. She saw the smoke, the fire engines and all the people gathered in front of Mrs. Borkowski's apartment building.

Above the chatter of the crowd, she heard Mrs. Borkowski's voice, shouting orders at the firemen.

Hanna panicked and hid behind a fence so that she wouldn't be seen by the landlady.

"She's in there. I know. I am certain," the landlady insisted.

"We've looked everywhere, Misses. There's no sign of anyone left in the building," the fire captain shouted.

"Go back," Mrs. Borkowski insisted. "You must order your firemen to go back inside and search for her. I tell you. There's a little girl still in the apartment on the third floor. Go back and look for a little girl with blonde hair."

Hanna felt her heart pounding in her chest. Little Hildie was still in the burning building. Her sister would be burned to death and it would be Hanna's fault for leaving the little girl in the house alone. Hildie probably woke up and started the fire. Hanna could no longer contain herself. She suddenly stood up and cried. "Oh no, Mrs. Borkowski, what's happened to Hildie?"

Mrs. Borkowsky caught sight of Hanna and came running toward her.

When she reached Hanna, she hugged the girl as tight as she could. "Hanna! Hanna! You're safe!"

"Is Hildie dead? Did she burn to death?" Hanna asked.

"No, Hanna. Hildie is just fine."

"Who are they looking for?"

"You, Hanna!"

"Me?"

"They couldn't find you. Where were you?"

Hanna was afraid to answer.

"I...I...I..." was the only word that could come out of her mouth.

Hanna didn't know what to say. Reluctantly, she asked, "Mrs. Borkowski, did Hildie start the fire?"

"The fire started in Mrs. Tagliano's apartment. The old lady must have fallen asleep with a cigarette in her hand. Hildie woke up and smelled smoke. She looked for you but couldn't find you. Because it was a little cooler today, I had decided to scrub the floor in the hallway. I was on my hands and knees when I smelled the smoke and heard Hildie knocking on the door. I ran up to get her. Gleason carried Mrs. Tagliano out of her apartment and alerted the others. He put out the fire as best he could. We got everyone out of the building but we couldn't find you."

The landlady paused to breathe a sigh of relief. "Thank goodness you got out in one piece."

Then she turned and called out to the crowd.

"It's a miracle! We found her. We found the little girl. She's safe. She got out all by herself."

She turned to Hanna. "The firemen have been searching for you since they arrived. How did you get out, Hanna?"

"Ummm," Hanna mumbled. After a moment, she answered. "I used the fire escape, Mrs. Borkowski. I got out through the fire escape like you told me. It was easy."

"What a smart and clever girl you turned out to be, Hanna." Mrs. Borkowsky was so happy Hanna was safe that she didn't ask her any more questions.

"Where's Hildie?" Hanna asked.

"They took her to Nativity House to get checked by the doctor. Come with me. Let me tell Gleason where I'm going and then I'll take you to her.

When Mama Myers learned there had been a fire in the neighborhood and people were gathering at Nativity House, she immediately called for her maid, Myrtle. Together they trudged down to Mr. Hong's Chicken Market. They waded through the sawdust on the floor and picked out five of his fattest chickens right from their cages. While Mr. Hong killed and plucked the chickens, they bought onions and carrots at the vegetable stall.

By five o'clock the comforting aroma of simmering chicken soup wafted through the rooms at Nativity House as tables were set and the reception room quickly turned into a dining hall prepared and ready to feed thirty people.

After dessert was served, the captain of the fire department arrived and gave his report. Everyone was relieved to hear that all the tenants were accounted for and that no injuries had occurred during the building evacuation. The fire captain reported that the fire had been contained to one apartment and that the building sustained only minor smoke damage. However because of the smoke, they declared the building uninhabitable until the end of the summer. Mr. Borkowski agreed that two months was exactly the amount of time he would need to clean and repaint his building.

A spirited discussion followed to determine which of the building's residents would need shelter and assistance. It quickly became obvious that many of the apartment building residents had family living nearly. After dinner they slowly dispersed to stay with their relatives.

As night approached, Marghereta Moratelli and Vilhemina Tatjana were the only ones left homeless with no place to sleep for the night.

"You can stay with me at my place on Bushwick Avenue. I have a big house and plenty of room," Mama Myers said.

"That is so generous of you, but how will I get to my job in the city?" Vilhelmina asked.

"Yes, I know, that is something to consider," Marghereta added. "Public transportation is not as accessible there, as it is in this neighborhood."

"I suppose we will make do," Vilhemina said.

Marghereta agreed. "Yes, we will wake up a little earlier and use our feet to walk to the trolley stop. However I'm afraid the boys will not be able to go to summer school if we are staying on the other side of town."

"I have another idea," Abe suggested. "We have a two-bedroom apartment above the daycare center."

"How will we decide who will use it?" Marghereta asked.

"We could draw straws," Vilhemina suggested.

"I was thinking the two women can share the apartment. Each family can have a bedroom of their own."

Marghereta hesitated and looked concerned. "What about mother?" She asked. "I am afraid she makes an awful lot of noise in the middle of the night. She often screams so loud that she wakes everyone up.

She needs a room all to herself. I suppose we can make do but she may keep everyone awake."

"I have a suggestion," Mama Myers said. "If I take Mrs. Tagliano with me, you two ladies can share the apartment. My house is big enough for her to have her own room and I have help in the evening. Quite frankly however, I wouldn't know what to do with her to keep her busy all day long."

"I have an idea. Perhaps she can spend time at the settlement house during the day," Angie suggested.

"If she could come here during the day, I will take her at night. I'll have Sam drive her to Nativity House in the morning and pick her up in the evening."

"Sounds like a perfect plan to me," Abe said.

Angie added, "I have one other idea. Mrs. Tatjana, as long as you will be living at Nativity House, will you allow your girls to attend our summer school program here?"

"Well, I suppose, Nurse Angie, if the girls want to go."

Vilhelmina Tatjana turned to her girls and asked them.

The girls clapped their hands and jumped up and down. "Yes, yes, Mama, please let us go!"

"Nurse Angie, I don't think I can say no to your request. The girls have decided."

Angie smiled. "Oh, Mrs. Tatjana, that makes me so happy. I am sure the girls will enjoy playing with all the other children. I know Maureen O'Shaughnessy will be pleased to hear your decision. I can't wait to tell her. She will be delighted that Hanna and Hilda will be going to summer school."

Chapter Twenty-Four

∾

August 13, 1926
Waldorf Astoria Hotel
The Steingold Suite
New York City

Wear sunscreen and bring an umbrella,
Be prepared for a change in the weather.

Harry and Adeline Steingold sat across from each other as their break-fast of Eggs Benedict, fresh blueberries, orange juice and coffee was served to them in the dining room of their penthouse suite.

"You look tired, Addie. Did the baby wake you last night? I didn't hear him."

"No, he slept through the night. I didn't sleep very well though. I kept waking up."

"Were you dreaming? Were you bothered by the war dreams again?"

"Yes, Harry. I'm afraid so."

"Why didn't you wake me up? We could have talked. You know that I would have listened."

"I didn't want to bother you. I wanted you to get a good night's sleep."

"Do you want to talk about it now?"

"I can't remember exactly what I dreamt. I know I was running, but you know what?"

"What, darling?"

"I don't want to dwell on the past today. I have a very special day planned. I've been looking forward to it all week."

"What are you going to do?"

"Today I'm taking Sadie to select her flower girl dress for Maureen's wedding. Angie and Leonora are joining us at Madame Renee's. She's the dressmaker who made Angie's wedding dress."

"Did Maureen also buy her wedding dress at Madame Renee's?"

"Yes, she went in March with her mother. It's going to be fun day. I'm excited because we are all going to get a sneak peek at Maureen's wedding gown. Madame Renee always puts together a special celebration when the bridal party comes to select their dresses. She is serving a light lunch...tea with tea cakes and cucumber sandwiches....very ladylike. I'm bringing Rachel."

"...and baby Henry?"

"Of course, why would I take the baby's nurse and not take the baby? I asked Rachel yesterday if she'd like to come. She said she'd love to go and was looking forward to riding out to Brooklyn in the Studebaker."

"Will you be out all day?"

"I think so. We have to select a dress design that pleases everyone. Then the ladies will get measured and fitted."

"Do I see Madame Renee designing a dress for you, too, in my crystal ball?"

"Why would you say that? I'm only the flower girl's mother, not the mother of the bride."

"I simply thought you might like to match Sadie."

"As a matter of fact, I was thinking of looking at Madame Renee's collection but both you and I know that I have plenty to wear."

"Do you think Henry can stay out all day without a nap?"

"We're bringing the baby carriage. Philip said it would fit right in the back seat of the Studebaker if we put the top down."

"Where's Rachel going to sit?"

"In the front seat with Sadie and me, the three of us will fit if Rachel holds Henry."

"Sounds like you've thought of everything. I know Sadie is going to have fun."

"She will. Harry, will you be working late tonight?"

"No, I'm planning on being home in time to have dinner with you and the children. That is, if I start getting ready to leave right now. Let me know when you have an idea of how long I should make Maureen's diamond necklace."

"I'll have the answer for you this evening. Maureen will be modeling her wedding dress for us. When she has in on, I'll ask her what kind of necklace she has in mind to wear. I don't think she would ever guess that we will be giving her a diamond necklace as a wedding present. She will be so surprised."

"Perfect. Well, darling, I've got to go if I want to come home early tonight," Harry said, as he got up from the table and kissed his wife. "Don't get up. Try to finish your breakfast. You haven't touched anything on your plate."

"I will, Harry. Hope you have a good day."

"See you tonight, darling."

When Adeline, Rachel and the children arrived at Madame Renee's Bridal Boutique, the ladies of the bridal party were relaxing on Madame's luxurious maroon mohair couches. Maureen's mother, Lillian O'Shaughnessy, and Angie were having tea at the tea table.

Madame Renee was overly gracious and attentive to Adeline.

"Ah, welcome, Mrs. Steingold! We are so honored by your presence this morning. Who are these adorable little angels accompanying you?"

"I would like to introduce Sadie, my beautiful daughter and this handsome lad is Henry, my son. This is Rachel, their nurse."

"Welcome! Welcome! Would you care for a bit of refreshment before we start the fashion show?"

"Perhaps a little later, Madame, I want to say hello to everyone first."

"Please make yourself at home. While you get comfortable and relax, I'll prepare my dresses for the showing."

After introductions, Madame Renee returned to the main room where the ladies were sitting. She lifted her hands above her head and clapped her hands.

"Attention! Attention! If everyone is ready, I should like to begin."

Madame Renee rolled out a cart. She presented three rolls of fabric.

She slowly unrolled the first one and held it up for everyone to see. "This is the peach-colored satin your mother and I have chosen for the dresses of the bridesmaids."

Maureen's mother asked, "What do you think, ladies?"

"It's gorgeous, Aunt Lillian," Cynthia, Maureen's cousin, answered.

Her sister Mary agreed, "I like it, too!"

"Good, I'm glad."

Madame Renee presented her second fabric selection to the group. "Now, for the maid-of-honor and our flower girl, may I suggest the same peach satin but with an overlay of this delicate Alisson lace on the skirt? Then envision, if you will, a large satin bow trailing to the floor behind our beautiful little flower girl."

Lillian O'Shaughnessy approved, "Very nice, Madame Renee, very nice, indeed."

Madame Renee spread out her third fabric choice and announced, "I would like to suggest his pale olive-green silk for you to wear, Mrs. O'Shaughnessy, as the Mother-of-the-Bride. I feel it would coordinate perfectly with the color of the bridesmaids' dresses, not to mention the flowers and the greenery."

"Yes, I like it very much."

Madame Renee smiled. She clapped her hands once again. "We will now begin. Here are a few of the styles I've chosen that I think you will adore." She turned toward the curtained stage. "Ladies, ladies, let us begin the fashion show."

One by one, six of Madame Renee's models dramatically paraded through the room, swirling their dresses around the ladies who were sitting down.

"These are a few of the more traditional styles I've created for today's fashionable bridal parties, but if you hold your breath for a moment, I shall present to you a more contemporary version of each dress that you, modern women, might prefer."

After much discussion, the bridal party selected a traditional empire-waist dress but with a shorter, more fashionable hemline.

"Splendid choice, ladies, I couldn't have made a better selection myself. May I suggest a light lunch before I take your measurements this afternoon?"

"That would be lovely."

"Come. Follow me. The luncheon table has already been prepared and is waiting for you."

Madame Renee led them into her dining room where they found a delightful lunch presented to them. There was a tea table covered in lace with delicate china teacups lined up in a perfect row. Six flavors of exotic teas from all over the world were offered aside matching pitchers of cream and tiny crystal bowls filled with lemon, honey and sugar. Assorted open-faced sandwiches, made with smoked salmon, herring, cucumbers and olive tapenade, were displayed on shimmering silver platters. Tiny petit-fours, crumpets with clotted cream and berry tarts were neatly placed on leaded-crystal plates.

"The table looks beautiful, Maureen," Leonora said, as she sat down.

Maureen turned to the others. "Come, let's all sit down. Leonora has some very exciting news to share with us."

Leonora looked surprised. "What? My news could wait. After all, this is your day, Maureen."

"Oh, how can you keep such important news a secret? This is a perfect time to tell everyone the latest development in your love life."

All eyes were on Leonora. "Well, if you must know..."

"What? Tell us. Did you meet someone? Don't keep us in suspense."

"Well," Leonora began but stopped when baby Henry suddenly started to cry.

Maureen ignored Henry's tears and stood up so that everyone could hear her. "They made up," she announced loudly.

"Who?"

"Alfonso and Leonora have made up. They made up two days ago. Leonora told me last night."

"Oh, Leonora, that's wonderful news," Angie said.

"How did it happen?" Cynthia asked.

"Tell us all the details," Mary added.

Adeline was about to sit down but she hesitated when she heard the baby cry again. She looked at Rachel. "He's hungry."

"Yes, and it's soon coming up to his naptime. I should like to feed him before he naps, Mrs. Steingold."

"Would you like to eat first, dear?"

"No, I will be quite all right. If it is okay with you, I'll just take him into the other room and feed him. Then I'll put him down for a nap. Perhaps I could take him for a walk in his carriage while the ladies are being fitted."

"That's a good idea, Rachel, but only on one condition. You sit down and have something to eat before you go outside. I'll start to feed Henry while you eat."

"Thank you, Mrs. Steingold, that's very thoughtful of you."

After lunch, while the ladies in the bridal party were being measured for their dresses, Rachel took Henry out for a stroll in his carriage. The rhythm of the moving carriage quickly lulled the toddler to sleep. Rachel feared he would wake up if she stopped the steady movement of the carriage. She walked more than twenty blocks before she realized she was too hot and tired to go on. When she passed Milano's Bakery, she longed for a cold cup of frozen lemon ice to cool her off.

Rachel peeked in and saw the baker was behind the counter. During the summer months, he would sometimes sit by the store window. If someone wanted ices, he would simply slide open the window and serve them his Italian ices through the window.

Rachel wondered if she should leave the toddler unattended. Baby Henry was sound asleep. She looked up and down the street. The street appeared to be deserted. No one was around. She usually didn't leave the boy alone, even for a minute, but it would only take a minute to buy a cup of lemon ice. Rachel put both the front and rear brakes on to prevent the wheels of the carriage from rolling. She left baby Henry sleeping safely in his carriage while she snuck into Milano's to buy ices.

Mr. Milano served her and she quickly paid. As she was leaving, Mrs. Milano came out from the kitchen and commented: "What a beautiful day it is today."

She asked Rachel, "Where are you off to on such a nice day?

Rachel politely answered her and hurried out of the store.

She knew something was wrong as soon as she stepped outside on the sidewalk. The baby's blanket was on the ground. Confused, Rachel picked it up. She looked around. She looked up and down the street. There was no one in sight. She was beginning to fold the blanket when she froze.

Then she screamed.

The carriage was empty.

"Help! Help! The baby is gone," Rachel screamed.

She ran back into Milano's Bakery. "Please, help me, Mr. Milano. The baby is gone. Call the police!"

Chapter Twenty-Five

Saturday, August 14, 1926
The Brooklyn Bugle
Front Page Article

EXTRA! EXTRA!
STEINGOLD BABY MISSING!
Article Written by Clarence Wilkins

Henry Randolph Steingold, 17-month-old adopted son of Harold and Adeline Steingold, has been missing since 1:41 pm yesterday afternoon, Friday, August 13th. There were no witnesses, and it is widely believed that the toddler has been abducted for a ransom. The toddler was last seen in front of Milano's Italian Bakery on Graham Avenue in the Williamsburg section of Brooklyn.

The baby's nurse, Rachel Zinzer, left the toddler sleeping in his baby carriage when she quickly went inside Milano's Bakery to purchase a lemon ice. When she returned, the toddler was gone.

"I only left him alone for a few minutes. Mr. Milano served me right away. I went out to the carriage as soon as I paid for my lemon ice. I didn't see anyone on the street."

Police were called to Graham Avenue immediately and responded to the child's disappearance within minutes. Throughout the afternoon, they questioned store owners, pedestrians and neighbors in and around the vicinity of Graham Avenue. No signs of struggle were reported. The motive for the kidnapping remains unknown.

The kidnapping has triggered a citywide search. The police commissioner has ordered extra foot-patrol policemen on duty. He has established a police hotline to report any suspicious activity and possible toddler sightings. Every lead will be investigated. Guards have been posted at all major highway crossings. All bus and railroad stations, as well as ferry terminals, have been alerted for travelers with young children.

The toddler weighs twenty-five pounds and has light brown hair and brown eyes. He was last seen wearing navy-blue cotton overalls, a white shirt and white shoes. The Steingolds are the owners of Steingold Jewelers. The family requests your prayers and vigilance. They are asking for anyone with information about the abduction to come forward.

Chapter Twenty-Six

August 14, 1926
Day One
The Waldorf Astoria Hotel
The Steingold Suite
New York City

They searched the city far and wide,
No clues or motives did they find.

Nurse Angie Goodwin felt helpless. There was nothing she could do except pray and stay close to Adeline to reassure her that everything would turn out all right. When Angie arrived at the Waldorf Astoria Hotel, the lobby was filled with policemen and reporters. No one was allowed up to the Steingold penthouse suite without a police escort.

The penthouse living room was filled with policemen and two plainclothes detectives, Detective O'Brien and his partner, Detective Cassidy. They questioned Adeline, Harry and Rachel, separately and together, throughout the day. Angie held Adeline's hand, hour after hour, as the investigation continued.

"Mr. and Mrs. Steingold, do you have any enemies that you know of?" Detective Martin O'Brien asked.

"None that I can think of," Adeline answered.

"Mr. Steingold, perhaps you remember an irate customer…someone who wasn't satisfied with their purchase at one of your stores. Can you recall anyone recently dissatisfied with a transaction?"

"The customer always comes first at Steingold Jewelers. If a paying customer has a problem with his purchase, we will repair or replace the item."

"Mr. Steingold, would you agree that it is quite impossible to please everyone one-hundred percent of the time?"

"Yes, of course, I agree with your statement."

"Therefore, you will admit that you have had one or two customers who were not completely satisfied with the service at your store."

"I agree that not everyone can be completely satisfied all the time."

"Can you remember at least one such person?" the detective persisted.

"No, no, I cannot. You have already questioned my employees."

"Do you keep records?"

"Yes, we have a record of all purchases on file."

"Do your employees keep a record of all complaints?"

"We have them also on file. As I told you, all complaints are addressed immediately and are corrected, either by replacement or repair."

"What if someone wanted their money back?"

"It is our store policy that we would refund the full amount of their purchase."

"That's a very generous policy, if I may say so."

"We have a reputation in the community, you know."

"So we can assume that neither you, nor Mrs. Steingold, have any known enemies. You know of no one who would want to hurt you or your child. Is that true?"

"As far as I know, detective, that is true," Adeline answered.

"Mr. Steingold, this is just a hunch. Have you ever used your children to advertise the products in your store?"

"Indeed not, why would I do that?"

"I try to cover every angle. That's what I do best. I was thinking along the lines that maybe the boy's picture was in a newspaper advertisement. Someone could have seen his photograph and targeted him as a rich kid who could bring in a hefty ransom."

"I see. No, I have never used my children in the store's ads."

"Therefore, we can rule that out."

"...But do you remember that newspaper article last January, Harry?" Angie asked.

"Yes, I remember that article. It was the day that the settlement house reopened," he replied.

"After the celebration at Nativity House, Clarence Wilkins wrote the front page article about it."

"Who is Clarence Wilkins?" Detective O'Brien asked.

"He's the reporter from *The Brooklyn Bugle*," Harry answered. "The photographer asked our permission to take a family photograph with the bishop. My wife was upset because Mr. Wilkins put our picture on the front page of the morning edition of the newspaper."

Detective O'Brien was interested. "Tell me more. Mrs. Steingold was upset with the newsman. Did she tell him? Did they have words?"

"No, I never talked directly to him," Adeline answered. "I was upset but I never told him. He chose to feature my family on the front page cover and not Angie and Abe Goodwin, who are the founders of Nativity House."

Detective O'Brien turned to Angie. "That's you, correct?"

"Yes, my husband and I started Nativity House," Angie answered.

Harry elaborated. "The settlement house held a reopening cele-bration in Brooklyn and invited everyone in the neighborhood. The bishop came and so did a reporter from *The Brooklyn Bugle*. He brought his photographer along who took pictures of the event. The morning edition of the paper featured a picture of the bishop with my family as the benefactors."

"...And your boy was in the photo, you say?" O'Brien asked.

"Yes, front page."

"What day was that exactly?"

"It was months ago, in January. I have a few copies of the article in the bedroom. I can take one out and show you."

"Yes, if you would...that would be helpful."

Adeline stood up and went into the bedroom. She searched through her desk for the manila envelope which held the copies of the newspaper article. When she found it, she pulled one out and brought it into the living room to show the detective.

Detective Martin O'Brien studied the photograph. "Very interest-ing...there's a possibility that someone saw this picture and targeted your family. Can I keep this?"

"Do you really think something like that could happen?" Adeline asked. "Of course, you can keep the newspaper clipping. I have others."

"We can't rule it out right now," the detective answered. "Mrs. Steingold, let me ask you another question. What did you do before you married Mr. Steingold?"

"I worked as a registered nurse."

"Where did you work?"

"I worked at Ellis Island Hospital."

"How long did you work there?"

"With the exception of my time in the military, I worked there for over ten years."

"You were involved in the war?"

"Yes."

"What did you do during the war?"

"I served as a nurse in a field hospital."

"Where were you stationed?"

"In France," Adeline answered.

"Did you run into any problems?"

"Every day, detective, there were dozens of problems every day. After all, there was a war going on in France."

"…And while you were working at Ellis Island Hospital, there must have been someone you disappointed…a patient not pleased with your care…a physician perhaps…or another nurse you offended?"

"No, sir, no one stands out in my memory."

"Surely in the ten years you worked at Ellis Island Hospital, there must have been someone disappointed in your care."

Angie spoke. "She's a good nurse, Detective O'Brien. I worked with her at Ellis Island Hospital. Her patients loved her."

"…And the staff?"

"We all got along. Of course, we had the usual misunderstandings but nothing that couldn't be resolved," Angie answered.

"Mrs. Steingold, tell me more about the governess you hired to care for your child? How much do you know of this woman named Rachel Zinzer?"

Harry answered. "I hired her. Her parents, Frederick and Mable Zinzer, have worked for my family for many years. They continue to do so. Rachel grew up in the Steingold household. I believe she wouldn't do anything to hurt our son."

"Are you absolutely certain? Isn't it possible that she may have developed a grudge toward your family during the many years her parents worked in servitude to them?" the detective asked.

Adeline looked at her husband.

"Haven't you questioned my parents' household staff?"

"We have, Mr. Steingold."

"Has anyone expressed dissatisfaction with their employment?"

"No one, but perhaps this young girl was disgruntled after a lifetime of watching her parents serve you and your family."

"Detective, we supported her through school. We provided room and board for the entire family. They have been loyal members of the household staff who have been paid handsomely for their services. They are employed by my parents. They don't live in servitude."

"Will you discharge Rachel Zinzer because of her irresponsible actions?"

Both Harry and Adeline looked at each other. "No!" They said in unison.

"I trust Rachel," Harry said.

"It was a mistake that could happen to anyone," Adeline added.

"...And you sincerely believe that the girl is not involved in a kidnapping plot in anyway?"

"I believe that," Harry answered. "You can see for yourself how upset she is. I don't have any reason to believe otherwise."

"So far, her record is clean. Let's go on then. Can you think of an unhappy store employee, perhaps someone upset about their job or their pay?"

"Detective O'Brien, you keep asking the same questions over and over again. I assure you that I have been racking my brain for an answer. We haven't come up with a clue."

"Well, let's take a break. My partner, Detective Cassidy, is working on a different angle. We've both been assigned to your case. He has a few questions for you."

Detective Cassidy came forward.

"Mr. and Mrs. Steingold, in light of receiving no request for a ransom in the past twenty-six hours, there is a possibility that your son may have been taken by someone who wishes to raise the child as their own."

"Is that really something you are considering?" Adeline asked.

"Since there is no ransom request and no evidence of an unaccounted toddler leaving the city limits, we must leave no stone unturned."

"...And what is it exactly that you are thinking?"

"When was the baby adopted?" the detective asked.

"We adopted Henry when he was two months old."

"What agency handled it?"

"As I told you before, it was a private adoption."

"Was this adoption legally recorded?"

"Yes, detective, our attorney worked directly with the mother."

"...And where is the mother now?"

"She is attending college. My attorney receives status reports of her progress regularly from the college."

"Why is that?"

"As part of the adoption arrangement, we offered to pay her college tuition."

"Yes, we know that. We've been to the school, checked the records and verified she is a student. They spoke highly of her and gave us her address. We've already interviewed her.

"Why are you bringing this up again?"

"Perhaps there was something we missed. You never know." Detective Cassidy scratched his head. "Let me ask you this. Do you know of any other woman in the neighborhood who was pregnant recently and lost the child?"

"I only know of one, detective. Visiting Nurse Maureen O'Shaughnessy knows the women in the neighborhood better than I."

"We questioned her already. She gave us a few names. She said there was a baby who died at Nativity House. Can you tell me about that incident, Mrs. Goodwin?"

"A mother brought her infant to us last spring. Her baby had died unexpectedly while he was sleeping in his carriage."

"…And you couldn't save him?"

"My husband, Dr. Abe Goodwin, tried but was unsuccessful in reviving the infant."

"…And the parents were angry with your husband?"

"No, in fact, they appeared most appreciative."

"We have assigned a plain clothes detective to follow all of them very closely."

"Are they suspects?"

"They are not above suspicion."

"Oh dear, I would hate to think such a thing."

"Sorry, but we do have to consider everything. Mrs. Goodwin, you mentioned you saw a man at the schoolyard across from the clinic. Is it possible he was spying on Mrs. Steingold?"

"I never considered that. I only mentioned it to you because I thought it was unusual for the man to often appear at the exact time the schoolchildren were dismissed from school but I never saw him leave with any of the children."

"What time of day did you see him?"

"I usually saw him standing by the courtyard between three and three-thirty in the afternoon."

"...And what exactly did he do."

"He appeared to be waiting. I first thought he was waiting for one of the schoolchildren but he never picked anyone up."

"Would you say that he was watching the comings and goings of the settlement house?"

"I never considered that. I thought he was watching the schoolchildren."

"Didn't you tell me that he stood directly across the street from Nativity House?" Detective Cassidy asked.

"Yes, but..."

"So he had a clear view of your establishment."

"I suppose you could say that. He just didn't appear..."

Harry Steingold interrupted the detective. "Detective Cassidy, you said you picked up the young fellow already."

"We have, sir."

"Then may I ask why you are bringing this up again?"

"We didn't get much information from him. He says he had nothing to do with the kidnapping, but we still have him in custody. I'm certain he'll spill the beans, sooner or later." The detective turned to Angie once again. "One more question, I just want to get this right. You said you saw the man standing across the street regularly but then you didn't see him for weeks at a time. However he recently started to spy on you again."

Angie corrected the detective. "I never said he was spying on us."

"I understand. Please, bear with me. This may be important. Did you see him on the day of the kidnapping?"

"No."

"Did you see him the day before the kidnapping?"

"Yes, that's when he first appeared again. It was after a month or two of not seeing him around. I remember thinking that it was a little odd that he suddenly appeared in the middle of summer when school was closed."

The questioning continued into early evening which caused Harry to be concerned. "Detective, can the ladies take a break? All this constant questioning is exhausting everyone. They haven't eaten their supper."

"Yes, of course, we should break for supper."

"Ladies, room service should be bringing up our food in a few minutes. Let's go in the dining room and have a late supper with Sadie before she goes to sleep. She's very upset," Harry said.

"Let's go," Angie agreed, standing up.

"Yes," said Adeline. "I know Sadie's upset. I want to be with her but I'm not feeling very hungry. I don't think I can eat a thing."

"You have to eat something, dear. You haven't eaten all day."

"I feel too sick to eat. My stomach is tied up in knots over all this."

"I know, Adeline, but you must force yourself to eat something. You have to be strong and healthy when Henry comes back home."

"Go ahead, folks. Go and have your dinner. That's all the questioning for tonight but I will be waiting right out here if you think of anything." Detective Cassidy thanked them for their time and waved them into the dining room. The doorbell rang. "I'll wager that's your food arriving right now."

While dinner was being served in the dining room, Detective Cassidy interrupted with a knock on the door. "There's a girl downstairs in the lobby. Says she wants to see you. She's a Miss Leonora Bartoli. Do you know her?"

"Yes, please send her up."

"Who is she?"

"She is a volunteer worker from the settlement house."

"I'm on it."

A uniformed policeman escorted Leonora up to the penthouse and handed her over to Detective Cassidy at the front door. She followed the detective into the dining room where Angie and the Steingolds were finishing up their supper.

"Here she is," the detective announced.

"Leonora, I'm so glad to see you. Does your father know you're out this evening?"

"I stopped at home first to ask him if I could come over. My father gave me his permission. I've been working at Nativity House all day, helping Dr. Abe. I stayed until after five."

"Why did you stay so late? Was the clinic very busy?"

"Just the usual, Angie, but don't worry, Dr. Abe had everything under control. He's handling everything. I left at three-thirty to meet Alfonso. I waited for him for over a half hour but when I realized he wasn't coming, I went back to the clinic to help Dr. Abe."

"You went all the way back to Brooklyn?"

"No, of course not, Alfonso has been meeting me at Nativity House. If he doesn't have an evening class, he comes to Johnson Avenue to meet me. He waits for me across the street. That way we get to spend time together on the train before I have to go home."

"Oh no!" Angie shouted.

Adeline asked, "Leonora, did Alfonso plan to meet you this afternoon?"

"Yes, at three-thirty but he wasn't there. I'm getting a little worried. When I stopped at his father's shop a little while ago, Mr. Ferrara said he went to college as usual this morning." Leonora looked concerned. "He hasn't been home. It's not like him to not show up someplace when he said he'd be there."

"Oh, no, Leonora!" Adeline said as she dropped her fork. "I think we have something to tell you."

"Come, quick!" Angie grabbed Leonora's hand.

"Where are we going, Angie?"

"To get Alfonso out of jail, he's being held downtown for questioning. I'm sorry to say this but if we don't hurry, I believe it will be my fault if Alfonso gets arrested."

Chapter Twenty-Seven

~

August 15, 1926
Day Two
Nativity Settlement House
Williamsburg, Brooklyn

Her idea started as the smallest seed,
Then it grew with the greatest speed.

Maureen kicked off her shoes and sighed, "I'm tired."

"I am, too, but they're all packed up now. Greta and Vilhemina are all ready to move back into their apartments tomorrow. It was nice of you to stay to help us get them packed and organized," Angie said.

Angie and Maureen were resting in their cozy back office at Nativity House.

"I can't believe Gleason Borkowski was able to get his building cleaned and painted so quickly."

Angie laughed. "He was very motivated. He was losing valuable rent money."

"Yes, you're right. He fixed the ceiling in Vilhemina's apartment and repainted all the apartments in less than six weeks."

"Vilhelmina told me that with the money she saved on rent, she's planning on cutting back and only working two evenings a week at the Roseland Ballroom."

"I'm so glad to hear that. She said that she enrolled the girls in Nativity School."

"They start their first day of elementary school the day after Labor Day."

"Did she ever tell you why she didn't enroll Hanna in school last year?"

"She said she wanted to send the girls to Catholic school but she was embarrassed that she didn't have the five dollars a month that they ask for tuition expenses for each child."

"Does she have it this year?"

"No, but she's paying half. She went to the rectory and spoke to Father Salvia about paying less. He agreed to enroll both girls if she would pay half the recommended tuition."

I'm glad something good came out of the whole thing." Maureen was quiet for a moment and then asked, "Angie, can I ask you something?"

"Yes, Maureen. What is it?"

"It's kind of important. I really want your opinion. I want to know what you think I should do."

"About what, Maureen?"

"Do you think I should postpone my wedding next month?"

"Why would you do that?" Angie asked.

"I don't know, Angie. How can I get married with Adeline's baby missing?"

"I'm certain the police will find him any day now."

"Henry has been missing since Friday. The police haven't come up with a clue. I can't help myself from thinking that this is my fault."

"How can it be your fault?" Angie asked.

"I planned the luncheon at Madame Renee's. If we didn't go for our dress fittings, Henry might still be with us."

"That's not true, Maureen. You aren't responsible in any way. Something like this could occur anywhere, anytime, any day."

"...But Adeline brought Henry and Rachel with her that day."

"Maureen, she sometimes brings her son with her to Brooklyn. She's brought Henry and Rachel to Nativity House a number of times to visit us this summer."

"I suppose you're right."

"You're much too hard on yourself, Maureen. You are not responsible for this in any way. You must believe that."

"I'll try, Angie. How's Adeline holding up?"

"Not great but that is to be expected. She's devastated, of course. I was with her all day yesterday. She's so sad and exhausted both physically and emotionally. She hasn't been eating. She says she feels nauseous. There are detectives and policemen in and out of her hotel suite, day and night. The detectives are constantly questioning her. They believe she holds the key to uncovering a clue as to Henry's whereabouts."

"Have they had any leads at all?"

"Not a one."

"What happened with Alfonso? Was he angry when you went down to the police station?"

"Alfonso doesn't have a mean bone in his body. No, he wasn't angry at all. He was so relieved that Leonora and I showed up at the station. He didn't have a clue as to why the police hauled him in for questioning. He certainly didn't know anything about the kidnapping, other than what Leonora told him. That fact made the police suspect him because of the connection to Leonora and Nativity House."

"Thank goodness, everything's cleared up now."

"When we realized what had happened, we hurried to tell Detective Cassidy. He went down to the station with us. Leonora told them the whole story. I verified it and they released Alfonso on the spot."

"What a mix-up that was."

"It surely was."

"...And you never recognized him when he was waiting across the street?"

"As I said, most of the time, he wasn't facing me. All I saw was his cap."

"I don't know why she never told me he was meeting her across the street. She could have told me."

"Well, she did tell us he met her after work."

"...But I thought he met her at the train station in the city."

"I thought that, too. Who would ever think he would take the train out to Brooklyn only to turn around and ride the train to go back to the city again?"

"People in love would," Maureen answered.

"Yes, they are in love. Leonora and Alfonso planned it that way so that they would have extra time together. Her father still doesn't know about them."

"When is she going to tell him?"

"Soon, I hope."

"What will happen now with the investigation?"

"The police are giving the kidnappers until today to make a ransom request. After today they will change their strategy."

"In what way, Angie?" Maureen asked.

"One train of thought is that the family photo in the newspaper called attention to the boy and targeted him as a child that would bring in a large ransom. The police believe that the kidnappers may have been spying on the comings and goings of the family for months. However if the baby wasn't kidnapped for ransom money, there may be another motive."

"Like what?"

"What if the Steingold family wasn't specifically targeted? Suppose anyone's toddler could have been abducted that afternoon. What if the boy was simply in the wrong place at the wrong time? Perhaps the kidnapper wanted a child for her own. She could be a mother who lost her child or a woman who can't have a child?"

"Seriously? Do you think?"

"Truthfully, Maureen, I don't know what to think. I don't have any answers. The police are actually keeping tabs on Henry's birth mother, as well as Nellie O'Donegan and her husband Francis."

"You mean that poor couple who lost their son in April?"

"Yes."

"They must be so upset."

"They don't know they are being followed. There are plainclothes detectives following them without their knowledge."

"Why?"

"They want to see what they are doing and where they are going. They are persons of interest and their actions might lead them to the baby. For example, the detectives might spy them buying baby cereal or diapers, things like that."

"Do you really think they had anything to do with Henry's kidnapping?"

"I don't believe the O'Donegan couple had anything to do with Henry's disappearance but the police have to consider everything I suppose. They are initiating a county-wide search tomorrow. They believe the child may still be in the borough of Brooklyn. They've already started going house to house."

"They can't search every building in Brooklyn. That's impossible."

"No, but they plan to check in with every superintendent and landlord. They are asking them if they know of a new baby living in the building."

"That's absurd."

"Is it? It sounds reasonable to me."

"Yes, it does. However, no one living in this neighborhood will talk to the police. You see, they don't trust anyone in uniform. They will never give the police any information about their neighbors. They are very protective of each other in that way. It goes back to the old country."

"So you don't think the police will get information from them."

"Have they gotten anything as yet?"

"No, they haven't a clue."

"That's because the people in this neighborhood will never tell their secrets to the police."

Angie agreed with Maureen. "They will only talk among themselves."

"That's right. They will only talk to each other and…"

"...And who?" Angie asked.

"...And to us, the nurses. They trust us. If we were asking questions about a new baby in the building, they would talk to us. They know that we have their best interests at heart."

"I agree. If I were to ask a landlord if there was a new baby living in his building, he might tell me because I was a nurse."

Maureen nodded in agreement. "He would tell you because he knows that you only wanted to help...perhaps get the baby vaccinated or teach the new mother how to take care of her baby. Angie, what if we were to go?"

"You and me, Maureen? We would never be able to go to all the apartment buildings in Brooklyn. It would take months."

"What if we had help?"

"Do you mean that we should assist the police in their investigation?"

"Yes, I am thinking of asking a few of my visiting nurse associates to come to Brooklyn. I could talk to Lillian Wald at Henry Street tomorrow before work. She might be able to release a couple of extra nurses to us for the day."

"You think she would lend us her visiting nurses to go undercover?"

"She might. It's worth a try, isn't it?"

"Yes, Maureen, it is."

"Oh, Angie, I think it could work. If only we can put it into motion."

"Maureen, I think if anyone can convince Miss Wald and the Henry Street visiting nurses to help Adeline, you could."

Chapter Twenty-Eight

~

Monday, August 16, 1926
The Brooklyn Bugle
Front Page Article

STEINGOLD BABY STILL MISSING!
Article Written by Clarence Wilkins

A citywide search continues for Henry Randolph Steingold, 17-month-old adopted son of Harry and Adeline Steingold. The toddler has been missing since Friday afternoon, August 13, 1926 when he was last seen by the child's nurse, Rachel Zinzer, in front of Milano's Italian Bakery on Graham Avenue in Brooklyn. The toddler was abducted when the nurse stepped inside the bakery to make a purchase. It is presumed that the child is being held for a ransom. However, at the time of this writing, no ransom has been requested by the kidnappers.

Police have established a telephone hotline to report any information about the toddler's whereabouts. Henry weighs twenty-five pounds and has light brown hair and brown eyes. He was last seen wearing navy-blue cotton overalls, a white shirt and white shoes.

The New York City police department has received a number of leads and reports on possible child sightings. Police are working night and day to follow up on every lead to solve the case as quickly as possible. The family is prepared to pay a sizeable reward for any information leading to the swift return of their child. They are asking for anyone with information about the abduction to come forward.

Chapter Twenty-Nine

～

August 16, 1926
Day Three
Henry Street Settlement House
New York City

The angels come to meet together
To find a way to help another.

Although the door of Lillian Wald's office at Henry Street Settlement House was open, Maureen O'Shaughnessy knocked before she entered.

The founder of the Visiting Nurse Service looked up from her desk.

"Ah, Miss O'Shaughnessy, how are you this morning?"

"I am fine, thank you. Do you have a few minutes, Miss Wald? May I come in and speak to you?"

"Certainly, I'll make time for you. You look worried, dear. What's on your mind?"

"Well, it's the Steingold kidnapping."

"Yes, I read about it in the paper. I meant to call Adeline long before this. I kept hoping the situation would be resolved and the child would appear."

"The whole family is devastated and most especially Adeline."

"She is such a good woman and a wonderful nurse. I don't know if you remember but she worked downtown as a visiting nurse many years ago."

"Yes, Miss Wald, she told me. She has been volunteering at Nativity House in Brooklyn where you assigned me on Tuesdays and Thursdays.

"I know."

"I feel so responsible."

"Why is that, dear?"

"The child was taken on the very day I invited Adeline to Brooklyn. You see, I asked Adeline's daughter, Sadie, to be the flower girl at my wedding next month."

"I didn't know that."

"We went for our dress fittings in Brooklyn. We were having lunch when Adeline's nurse took Henry for a walk. That's when the baby disappeared."

"…But you aren't responsible in any way."

"I know but I feel…"

"I can only imagine."

"Here's what I came to talk to you about."

"What is it?"

"Contrary to what you read in the daily newspaper, the police have come up with absolutely nothing. They have no leads, and there's been no request for a ransom."

"Go on, dear."

"The police believe the toddler could still be in Brooklyn. They are going house to house to search for him."

"Do they intend to search every apartment in Brooklyn? How can they do that?"

"They can't, Miss Wald. They are only questioning the landlords, superintendents or building janitors. They are asking them if anyone in the building has a new baby. So far the police haven't come up with anything."

"Of course, the immigrants out there often don't trust the police with that kind of information. Word on the street is that they won't tell their secrets to men in uniform for fear some information could be used against them. They are frightened that they could be deported."

"That's exactly what I said when Angie told me their plan."

"They may be wasting precious time."

"Yes, Miss Wald, I was thinking that the immigrants trust us, the visiting nurses."

"We've earned that reputation. I agree. They do trust the nurses. They know we're only here to help them."

"I had an idea that if the visiting nurses went house to house and asked the exact same questions the police are asking, they might be able to get the information the police are looking for."

"You're absolutely right. What are you proposing?"

"I was wondering if you could spare a group of visiting nurses for a day. We could all go out to Brooklyn to investigate and see if we come up with any leads."

"Do you think it would work?"

"I do, Miss Wald. I know the people out there. They will talk to us."

"I believe you, Maureen."

"This would have to be organized very quickly. Time is of the essence."

"We could call a meeting. We could ask for volunteers."

"It can only be one day. I can't spare my nurses more than that."

"One day is better than nothing. Do you think we could do it tomorrow?"

"That doesn't give us much time, does it?"

"No, but I think if we work together, we can do it. Nurse Angie Goodwin from Nativity House said she would help."

"I will ask the nurses to triage their neediest patients. I could send some out to Brooklyn to investigate and ask the others if they would double up on their home visits tomorrow."

"Would you?"

"Of course, I would. Adeline's one of our own. I think we should call for an all-hands emergency meeting this very evening, don't you?"

Chapter Thirty

❧

August 17, 1926
Day Four
Williamsburg, Brooklyn

In their quest to help another,
The angels search for a mother.

Visiting Nurse Veronica Turnbull was so excited about the mission that she had volunteered for the night before that she woke up an hour before her alarm clock rang and jumped right out of bed. She wanted to get an early start on the day because she had lots of ground to cover in Williamsburg. After a hasty breakfast of oatmeal and coffee, she dressed quickly in her summer navy-blue and white uniform and was out on the street before seven-thirty.

The morning air was cool, crisp and clear, reminding her of the autumn weather soon to come in September. In fact, the weather was so cool that she ran back to her apartment to grab her navy-blue uniform sweater. Although she might not need a sweater during the day, she thought it best to carry it with her because she expected her day to be a long one, and it could get chilly in the evening.

Veronica waited at the trolley stop anticipating an interesting day. The night before at the all-hands emergency meeting at Henry Street Settlement House, Lillian Wald and Maureen O'Shaughnessy had explained to the visiting nurses all the details of the search plan.

Veronica was the first nurse to raise her hand when Lillian Wald called for volunteers. Twenty-two other nurses followed, offering to rearrange their schedules and change their shifts in order to go out to Brooklyn the next day. Including Angie Goodwin and Maureen O'Shaughnessy, the total number of "nurse-detectives" had reached twenty-four.

The plan was well thought out and organized. The nurses' instructions were to report any lead they came upon or any suspicious activity they heard about directly to the police. If they actually got the name of a likely suspect, they were not to attempt to intervene with that person in any way. Lillian Wald and Angie Goodwin had spent the afternoon studying a map of the streets of Brooklyn around Milano's bakery. They divided the area into two dozen possible search routes. Each nurse received a map with written directions about her territory and the location of the nearest police station within it.

The nurses listened attentively to all the directives. The nurses were to travel alone and were told not to congregate in groups because this could cause suspicion. Arrival times were to be staggered. Each nurse was given a fifteen-minute window for her assigned arrival to her territory. "Act as if it's a normal work day. Do the ordinary things a visiting nurse does as she travels from one home to another." They were to ask landlords, building superintendents, cleaning ladies or janitors if there were new babies living in their building. If someone were to ask them why they were inquiring, their instructions were to pull out the Nativity House flyer that Nurse Angie Goodwin had prepared in advance. The flyer announced a series of new-mother classes at the Nativity Settlement House scheduled for the month of September.

Armed with her map and the Nativity House class announce-ments, Veronica stepped off the trolley and began her quest on the first block in her territory.

By ten-thirty in the morning, things weren't going according to her plans. In two hours, she had only covered one square city block. She realized she would have to work a great deal more efficiently if she was ever going to complete her assignment by the end of the day.

Veronica lost a great deal of precious time talking to the people in the neighborhood. When she appeared on the street, they would often stop her and bombard her with their concerns.

"No, I don't know of any new babies in the building, but, nurse, could you stop a minute and take this splinter out of my finger. I'm certain it will only take a minute of your time."

"I haven't heard a sound. The landlord says the walls in these apart-ments are a foot deep. They're almost soundproof, you know. Can I ask you a quick question, nurse? What should I do about my sciatica?"

"Wait a minute. Don't go away so fast. I got stung by a bee yester-day and it's still hurting me. Is that normal?"

"I think my son needs glasses. Does the Brooklyn Eye and Ear Clinic make eyeglasses for children?"

"Nurse, can you help me across the street? My mother told me to ask someone to cross me."

Whatever made her think this day would be any different from any other day?

On an ordinary workday in her assigned neighborhood, Veronica always made time to answer anyone who stopped her for advice. She was always happy to give instructions and directives about healthcare.

If she couldn't answer their questions, she directed them to a nearby clinic.

Veronica tried to be as patient as possible with the many inquiries she was receiving, but she felt herself getting more and more impatient when she was interrupted on every street corner.

This caused her to wonder. *I wonder if everyone is having this problem today. I won't be able to cover my territory by this evening. I'll never discover any clues about the missing child at this pace.*

By one o'clock in the afternoon, her apprehension mounted. She had only covered one-third of her assignment. She was both discouraged and hungry. Veronica forced herself to take a lunch break, arguing with herself all the way to Graham Avenue. She knew she didn't have much time to waste but felt she couldn't go on without stopping to eat and use the restroom. At the counter of Werner's Jewish Delicatessen, she ordered a hot potato knish and a glass of iced tea. After she paid for her meal, she carried her tray to a wooden table near the window. She spread a touch of tangy mustard and sprinkled sea-salt on her warm knish before biting into it. The creamy softness of the mildly-spiced mashed potato mixture that was folded inside a crisp golden coating comforted her. She ate the knish slowly, savoring each tasty mouthful. When she was finished, she felt ready to go on with renewed determination. The only way to make a dent in her hefty assignment was to walk a little quicker and to avoid eye contact with the people on the street. If someone stopped her, she would excuse herself by telling them she was rushing to an emergency house call.

At four o'clock, she reached a block of wooden row houses. Veronica counted a dozen houses that looked identical and thought they might be under the same management. She breathed a sigh of relief, thinking that she would only be required to locate one contact person. Unfortunately, this was not the case. She soon learned that although the houses were once owned by a single landlord, they were now individually owned. Therefore she would have to go into each house on the block.

When she reached the third building, Veronica climbed up the steep outside staircase and found the front door was locked. After studying the doorbell panel to the left of the front door, she selected the doorbell that was labeled *GFR*, Ground Floor Rear, because it didn't have a tenant's name assigned to it.

"Who is it?" A gruff voice came through the speaker.

"It's Visiting Nurse Veronica Turnbull, sir."

"What do you want?" he asked.

"I'm here to ask you a few questions."

"About what, may I ask? Are you from the city?"

"No, sir, I'm simply a visiting nurse from the settlement house."

"Wait there," he instructed. "I'll send my wife out to talk to you."

The front door opened. A little lady, no more than five feet tall, came out wearing a green floral cotton apron over her housedress. She had pink curlers in her hair.

"What can I do for you, dearie?"

"I'm Visiting Nurse Veronica Turnbull, Mrs..."

"Mrs. Weiss, Miss."

"Well, Mrs. Weiss. I work at the settlement house down the street. We're starting a series of new classes in two weeks. We'd like to invite the new mothers in the neighborhood to attend. Do you know anyone in your building who has a new baby?"

"No, honey, no one living here has a newborn, but…" Mrs. Weiss stopped mid-sentence.

"…But, what? May I ask you what you were going to say?" Veronica asked.

"I don't think this counts but I had a new tenant move in this weekend with a little toddler boy. She said her husband would be joining her any day. Funny thing, though, is that he's never showed up. The little fellow must miss his daddy terribly because he's been crying every day since they moved in."

"Really? That must put a terrible strain on you and the other tenants."

"Yes, the tenants have started to complain. They told me that they could hear the child crying all night."

Veronica frowned. "Poor little thing," she said.

"Yes, all that crying was bothering everyone so I went up this morning to see if I could help the lady. I knocked on the door but she didn't let me in. She came out into the hallway and told me the little boy is teething and missing his daddy. I suggested a teething cracker for him. I offered to go and buy him an arrowroot cookie to chew on. She tells me not to bother and says she has everything she needs. That seemed strange to me. I don't know if the new mothers' class would help her, seeing the child is a toddler and not a newborn, but if you ask me, she looked stressed. Maybe you can do something to help her. She doesn't look like she's managing very well."

"What apartment is she in?" Veronica asked.

"She's up there on the third floor, front, studio apartment. It's two flights up. Why don't you go up now and check on her?"

"I don't hear any crying."

"The little one must have tired himself out from crying so much. Perhaps he fell asleep. He doesn't stay asleep very long, though. Mark my words, he'll be awake in a few minutes time and will start his crying all over again."

Veronica thanked the lady as she turned to leave. "Thank you, Mrs, Weiss."

"Where are you going, honey? I thought you might like to go up and see if you can do anything to help."

"Yes, of course, I will be back to see her in a few minutes. I have to check on something important first but I will return. I promise."

"Okay, honey, go do what you have to do. Ring the bell when you come back and I'll let you in."

Veronica tripped as she backed down the long flight of stairs but was able to regain her footing when she turned around. Waving *goodbye* to the landlady, she started to walk away very slowly.

She took a deep breath to calm herself. *Walk slowly, Veronica. Act as if nothing is wrong.*

Veronica stopped and took out her map. The closet police station was only three blocks away. When she turned the corner, she started to run. She ran the whole three blocks and didn't stop until she reached the station.

Once there, she hurried up the steps and rushed through the double doors of the police station.

"I have something to report about the Steingold kidnapping case." She told the on-duty police sergeant at the front desk.

Chapter Thirty-One

August 17, 1926
Later That Evening
The Waldorf Astoria Hotel
The Steingold Suite
New York City

Her little girl is filled with fear,
She hopes and prays and sheds a tear.

A uniformed policeman stood guard at the entrance of the Steingold penthouse suite on the top floor of the Waldorf Astoria Hotel. Two plain-clothes detectives sat in the living room, patiently waiting for any communication from the kidnappers.

Harry heard Sadie crying in her bedroom. "Sadie's still awake. She's very upset, Adeline."

Adeline was pacing, walking back and forth from her bed to her bureau. "She was sleeping when I left her room. I stayed with her until she fell asleep."

"She must have awakened again."

"I don't know what to do, Harry. I sat with her for an hour, singing and reading stories. She doesn't want to be alone. Should I bring her in here?" Adeline asked with a frown of concern on her face.

"I think so, dear. I'll call the concierge to bring up a cot. She could sleep in here with us." He picked up the telephone to call the front desk.

"Good, I'm glad you agree. It will make her happy. I'll go and tell her."

"Is everything okay, Mrs. Steingold?" the detective asked as Adeline passed through the living room to reach Sadie's room.

"Everything's fine, detective, I'm going to bring my daughter into our bedroom," Adeline said as she reached Sadie's bedroom door.

She opened the door to find Sadie sitting up in bed, crying.

"Sadie, darling, are you all right?" Adeline asked as she turned on the bedside table lamp.

"No, Addie. I'm scared."

"You're safe, Sadie. There are policemen guarding us, inside and outside of this hotel."

"I'm scared for baby Henry."

"You're not the only one, darling. We're all upset."

"I miss my baby brother."

"I miss him terribly, too."

"I wish he would come back, Addie."

"The police are trying to find him to bring him back to us."

"We might never see him again."

Adeline reassured Sadie. "We must try to be hopeful. We must have hope and think the best."

"Baby Henry could die, you know."

"Why do you say that?" Adeline asked.

"Addie, remember when my mother left and disappeared?"

"Of course, I do. That's when I met you."

"My mother never came back. She died. The policeman told me."

"Yes, I know. It was an accident."

"Henry could have an accident. What if the people who stole him don't take good care of him? What if they drop him or something?"

"I have to believe he's okay and the police will find him soon."

"Do you think the kidnappers will try to steal me, too, Addie? If they do, maybe they will take me to Henry and I can save him."

"I promise you that you're safe, Sadie."

"Are you sure? Are you positive?" Sadie asked.

"There are policemen assigned to protect us night and day. There are two detectives sitting right outside in the living room. There's even a policeman standing by our front door, guarding the entire apartment. We're safe. We're all safe. Nothing will happen to us. Listen, Sadie, I have an idea. How would you like to sleep in the room with Harry and me tonight?"

"Yes, Addie. I'd like that."

"Come on then, let's go."

Sadie jumped out of bed and took hold of Adeline's hand.

"Harry ordered a little cot for you. They'll be bringing it up shortly. You can sleep in my bed while we wait for it to arrive."

Adeline and Harry tucked Sadie into the big double bed and sat on each side of Sadie.

"Sadie, we know you're sad. Addie and I are, too," Harry told Sadie.

"Why did they have to take our baby?" Sadie asked.

"We don't know. The police are trying to find out."

"When are they going to bring him back to us?"

"I wish I knew, dear," Harry said.

"Isn't there something you can do, Uncle Harry?"

"Everyone's doing everything they can. We have to be patient."

"…And brave," Adeline whispered as she started to cry.

"Now, now, dear, we must be strong." Harry leaned over and kissed his wife, wiping away a tear. Then he kissed Sadie on the forehead. "Maybe you could try to get some sleep, little lady."

"I can't. I just can't," Sadie moaned.

"How about we sing a song together? Let's sing the row-your-boat song."

"Can I say a prayer for Henry first like the sisters at school taught me?"

"Of course, dear, of course you can."

Sadie crawled out of the big bed and kneeled down. She folded her hands.

"Please, God, please bring baby Henry back to us. Please keep him safe. I love baby Henry with all my heart. I promise to always be good. I promise to listen to my teachers in school. I promise to listen to Uncle Harry and Addie every day. Please find a way to send my little brother back to us."

"That's a good prayer, Sadie."

"I think maybe we shouldn't be calling Henry a baby anymore," Sadie said.

"You're right. He's really not a little baby. He's growing, isn't he?"

"When he comes back, I'm gonna call him just plain Henry."

"That's a good idea. I think I will too."

Harry agreed. "Me, too, and when Henry comes back, I'm going to get busy to find a house for all of us to live in"

"You mean a real house with a fence and a garden?" Sadie asked.

"Yes, I think that we should be living in a house and not a hotel. We'll be safer in our own home. Would you like that, Sadie?"

"Yes, I think that's a good idea, don't you, Addie?"

"I do. We said we were going to start looking at houses last year. How can it be that a whole year has passed and we're all still living at the Waldorf?"

"Let's make a pact to move before the year ends."

Adeline agreed. "I'll make that deal. Sadie, come back into bed now."

Sadie climbed up and wriggled under the covers. Harry and Adeline began to sing. They went through three songs before Sadie put her head down on the pillow. As she was closing her eyes, she was awakened by a loud disturbance coming from the living room.

"I suppose the cot has arrived," Harry said, getting out of bed and going to the door.

The noise outside their room escalated as the policemen began to shout and cheer.

Puzzled about the commotion, Adeline asked. "Why are they so excited about a cot arriving?"

"Maybe it's something else…" When Harry opened his bedroom door to investigate, he stood face-to-face with Detective Cassidy.

Detective Cassidy was carrying little Henry on his shoulders.

"Look who's come home to you!" The detective announced.

"My baby!" Adeline jumped out of bed and ran to the detective as the toddler reached out his arms for his mother. Adeline grabbed her son and hugged him.

Harry put his arms around Adeline and Henry. "Thank the Lord. Thank the Lord."

Sadie popped up from her pillow. "God listened. He answered my prayer."

"Where did you find him?" Harry asked the detective.

"A woman had him in her apartment in Brooklyn."

"Oh, my! Who?"

"The woman gave her name as Penny Gibbs or something like that. You know her, Mrs. Steingold?"

"I never heard the name before."

"She says she knows you."

"How did you find him?"

"We didn't, the nurses found him."

"How?"

"Well, unbeknownst to us, the Henry Street nurses got together and developed a plan. Did you know anything about that?"

"No, they didn't tell me anything. What did they do?"

"They called a meeting last night and asked for volunteers to go out to Brooklyn and investigate."

"...But the police were investigating," Harry said.

The detective explained. "Yes, we were doing our best. We had the whole force out looking for the child but the nurses...they felt the people in the neighborhood would talk more freely to a nurse than a policeman in uniform. They said the people trusted the nurses."

"...And?"

"The nurses decided to take matters into their own hands, like guardian angels, they were. They divided up and went out investigating today."

"Really?"

"...And what do you know?"

"What?

"They went out announcing to everyone in the neighborhood that they were starting new mothers' classes at the settlement house. They

185

even mimeographed flyers to announce the classes. While they were going around town, they found out about a lady who moved into a studio apartment with a little boy over the weekend. Do you believe that? Looks like those guardian angels knew what they were talking about. Why, they did a faster job of investigating than we did. After one nurse told this landlady about the classes, the landlady said she had a tenant in her building who needed help. She said the woman's baby cried night and day."

"Poor Henry."

"So the nurse ran as fast as she could and rushed into the police station to report this information to us. Earlier this evening, we went to the apartment and sure enough..."

"What?"

"We found the little guy right there in the apartment with the lady. The lady didn't give us a fight or nothin'. She simply handed the baby over to us. 'Here he is. You can have him back.' That's what she said and she gave us little Henry."

"Who is she?"

"As I told you, she said her name was Penny Gibbs. They took her downtown. My partner, Marty O'Brien is questioning her now. I'm going down to meet him in a little while. As soon as we know anything, we'll pass it on to you. In the meantime, here's your little fellow."

Chapter Thirty-Two

August 1926
Police Headquarters
Brooklyn, New York

To take a child may be a sin and
It won't relieve the pain within.

At police headquarters, the questioning of suspect, Miss Penelope Gibbons, continued through the night.

"I didn't mean to do it, officer. You've got to believe me."

"Why'd ya do it, sister?"

"I don't know. Something came over me. I couldn't help myself."

"Let's start at the beginning. You emigrated from England last year."

"Yes."

"That was in November of 1925. Is that correct?"

"Yes."

"At the time of your emigration, you traveled as Penelope Gibbons. Is that correct?"

"Yes."

"Is that your real name?"

"Yes."

"Why did you change your name?"

"I didn't. Penelope Gibbons is my legal name. I only shortened my first name from Penelope to Penny. It sounded more modern, more American, don't you think?"

"How do you know the Steingold family?"

"I only know Mrs. Steingold. I knew her by her maiden name, Adeline Ferme'."

"What was your relationship with Mrs. Steingold?"

"We were in the war together. We were stationed in France near the town of Le Treport. I was a nurse's aide, a *VAD*."

"A what?"

"A *VAD*...V-A-D."

"What's a *VAD*?"

"V-A-D stands for volunteer auxiliary detachment. I was a volunteer nurse's assistant."

"You were a volunteer? Did you get paid for your service?"

"Yes. All *VAD*s received a monthly stipend."

"How long were you stationed in France?"

"Four years..."

"...And you worked with Mrs. Steingold during that whole time?"

"No, the American forces arrived in 1917. They took command of a number of hospitals that the British military had previously established. That's when I was assigned to work under Miss Ferme'. She was an American officer in charge of the British *VAD* contingent at the hospital."

"Okay, I get it. Would you say she was a good leader?"

"Yes."

"Was she cruel or unfair to anyone under her command?"

"No, sir."

"After all these years, why would you want to come to America to steal her baby?"

"I didn't come to steal her baby. I came to America for a fresh start."

"What were you running from?"

"I wasn't running from anything. I was trying to find happiness."

"And you wanted a kid?"

"No, it was nothing like that. You see, my parents are very protective. I was living with them in England. They would not allow me to work. I wasn't married. I am, what some call, a spinster lady. I wanted to branch out on my own."

"So you came here to America and, may I ask, what were your intentions? What was it exactly that you planned to do in America?"

"To work, save money and gain some training in my field. Eventually, I planned to return to England and buy a dress shop in London."

"Did you get a job?"

"I did."

"What kind of work do you do?"

"I work as a dress designer's apprentice."

"In a clothing factory?"

"No, I currently work for a private designer in Brooklyn. I studied art and clothing design at the university in London. Everything was working out fine."

"What happened?"

"It all started one morning when I was reading the newspaper last winter. I opened up the paper and saw a picture of a beautiful family on the front cover. I read the article. This was the family of a rich businessman who donated money to a health center. As I looked at the picture, something about it was familiar. I studied the picture and recognized Miss Ferme'."

"The same Miss Ferme' who was your superior officer in France?"

"Yes."

"...But you said she was fair to you."

"I didn't say that."

"What exactly was your beef with her?"

Penelope looked down and was silent.

Moments later, she began to speak. "You see, I was with child. I had gotten pregnant while I was stationed in France. I was going to have a baby and I wasn't married. I wasn't *that* kind of girl but I fell in love with an army sergeant during the war. After he was transferred, I learned I was pregnant. I kept it a secret for as long as I could. As the months passed, I had no choice but to report it to my superior officer."

"...And Miss Ferme', I mean Mrs. Steingold, did she ridicule you?"

"No, she never made me feel inferior or tainted."

"What did she do?"

"She sent me home, shipped me back to England on the next train leaving for Calais."

"That was a good thing, wasn't it?"

"No, I begged her not to send me home. I pleaded with her for more time."

"Why was that?"

"My parents had their station in the community to consider. They would be tarnished forever by a public scandal. I was certain that they would force me to abort my baby. Days later, I learned that my sergeant had been wounded. I submitted a request to remain at base camp a few more weeks. I wanted to be there in the event that the sergeant came through with a *field ambulance convoy*."

"Mrs. Steingold wouldn't let you stay."

"She sent me home. Soon after, I learned my sergeant died."

"That's when you planned your revenge."

"No, I never planned any such thing. I went on as best I could. Although it haunted me, I tried to forget the past. Ten years later, I was looking for a fresh start. That's when I decided to come to America."

"To get even…"

"No, to get ahead, I only wanted to get ahead. I wanted to learn the best of the fashion trade from Madame Renee."

"Did you?"

"Yes, I was working at Madame's when Miss Ferme'…"

The detective corrected her. "Mrs. Steingold…"

"Yes, Mrs. Steingold came last week to Madame Renee's Bridal Boutique, driving up in her fancy new Studebaker. She had her children and their nurse with her. She looked like every little thing is going her way. She's married to a handsome man, is rich, pretty and has two gorgeous children. Madame Renee is all over her, bowing and catering to her. It was disgusting how Madame fussed over the lady because of her money."

"That made you angry?"

"I felt it was unfair. She had everything. I had nothing. She was the reason I had lost everything. What got me even angrier is that when I came out to model my dress design, do you know what she did?"

"What?" the detective asked.

"She didn't even recognize me. I looked her straight in the eye, too. She didn't show even a hint of recognition. That's when it happened…"

"What happened?"

"The feeling that came over me."

"What feeling was that? Anger? Revenge?"

"I've been struggling for over ten years. During all that time, she hadn't given me one bit of a thought. She didn't even remember me or what she did to me. She was too busy living her uptown life, enjoying her riches with people waiting on her hand and foot. By lunchtime, I felt so hot and bothered that I couldn't breathe. I went outside for some air. As I standing by the employee entrance, I saw the baby nurse come out through the front door of Madame Renee's with the little boy in his baby carriage. I started following them. I had no intention of stealing the baby. When the nurse left him outside the store all alone, well, as I told you, something came over me, something fierce like I wanted to hurt Mrs. Steingold like she hurt me. I didn't even want her little boy but I knew it was the one thing she took from me and that would make us even."

"So what happened?"

"When the nurse was in the store, I snatched up the baby and started walking. I walked for a long time, trying to think of what I was going to do next. I was about to take the boy to my apartment but thought better of it. As I was walking with him, I saw a vacancy sign. I rang the bell and the landlady came out. She showed me this furnished studio ready to move in. I offered to take it, right there and then."

"Did you return to work?"

"No, I used the payphone at the Rexall Store to call Madame Renee. I told her secretary that I felt sick that afternoon"

"How did you plan to care for the baby? Who would care for the boy when you went to work?"

"I didn't think that far ahead. I remember thinking I would use the dresser drawer as a crib for him. Later that evening, I took the boy out again before the stores closed. I went back to Rexall's to buy rice cereal and diapers. I also bought a newspaper. The little guy was fine until we returned to the apartment. He wouldn't go to sleep. I guess he wanted his mother. He started crying and wouldn't stop. All his crying nearly drove me crazy. When he finally did fall asleep, I began to think a little clearer. I wanted to bring the baby back but, with the whole city looking for the kid, I didn't know how to get rid of him."

Chapter Thirty-Three

The Following Evening
The Waldorf Astoria Hotel
The Steingold Suite
New York City

To begin to heal a broken heart,
Forgiveness is the place to start.

That evening Nativity Health Clinic closed early. When summer school ended for the day, Dr. Abe and Nurse Angie put a sign on their door, borrowed Sam's car and headed into the city to visit Adeline and Harry.

When they arrived at the Waldorf Astoria Hotel, the lobby was quiet. Only one uniformed police guard stood sentry at the front door of the Steingolds' penthouse apartment.

"Good evening, officer. May we go in?" they asked.

"Good evening, folks, I'm Officer O'Hara. I'll have to announce you. Please show me your identification."

"Certainly," Angie said, searching through her purse for her wallet.

Abe pulled out his identification before Angie. The policeman studied their papers. "Please wait out here a moment," he instructed.

Angie and Abe waited in the hallway while Officer O'Hara obtained permission for them to visit the Steingolds.

Adeline came to the door with the policeman. "Angie, Abe, I'm so happy to see you."

"Harry called us this morning. We came as soon as we closed the clinic this afternoon."

"Angie, I can't believe it's over. Henry's here with us. He's safe."

"Adeline, we were overjoyed when we heard the news," Angie said, giving Adeline a kiss and a hug.

"We're so relieved," Dr. Abe added.

"We are too, Abe, the last five days have been a nightmare for us."

"I can only imagine."

"Angie, you didn't tell me the nurses were going out in full force to help us."

"I didn't want to disappoint you. Maureen came up with the idea. We didn't know if we would uncover anything."

"Come in. Tell me. How did you organize such a thing so quickly?"

"After Maureen talked to Lillian and Lillian agreed to the plan, we all got down to work. There were a million things to do. Leonora and Alfonso designed the flyers for the classes. Sam took them to be mimeographed. Abe helped us map out the territory."

"We didn't want to get your hopes up. You had enough to worry about," Abe said.

"I was shocked when I heard that it was the nurses who found Henry."

"No one hesitated a minute when Miss Wald presented the idea to her nurses. Everyone wanted to go. Some stayed behind in the city and doubled up on their home visits."

"I will be forever grateful for what they did and for what you both did. Thank you, my dear friends."

"No thanks necessary. We had to do anything we could to find Henry. We know how much you love him."

"He means so much to us. We're so lucky that he's home and he's safe. We are overflowing with gratitude. Angie and Abe, sit down, I have more news to tell you."

Adeline looked at Harry. Harry nodded approval. "We have something to tell you. It's good news. We've been doubly blessed."

"What is it?" Angie asked.

"Angie, Abe, you aren't going to believe this but this morning I learned that I am pregnant."

"Really? That's the best news I've heard all week. It's absolutely wonderful news. How did you learn you were pregnant?" Angie asked.

"Harry was worried that I wasn't eating and sleeping. He feared a tuberculosis recurrence. Everyone told him that it was to be expected under the circumstances. I thought so, also. I thought I felt nauseous because I was so upset about Henry. Harry wanted to be certain and sent for the hotel doctor yesterday. The doctor came and examined me. After I told him what I was feeling, he said he suspected something and wanted to take a blood test. He called this morning to tell me the results of the test showed that I was pregnant."

Angie couldn't contain herself. She jumped up and hugged Adeline again. "Oh, Adeline, I'm overjoyed."

Sadie ran into the room. When she saw Angie, she threw her arms around her. "Hi, Aunt Angie, I'm so happy."

"We all are, Sadie. Thank the Lord."

"I did, Aunt Angie, I did thank Him. I prayed to Him and He brought my brother back. I remembered to thank Him this morning."

"Oh, Sadie, I'm so proud of you."

Abe asked Harry. "How is Henry doing? Is he having any problems?"

"He was very happy to see all of us last night. However I think he was a little angry this morning. He's acting as if it was our decision to leave him with the woman. He may very well think that we gave him away. Do you think that's possible, Abe?"

"That makes sense to me. He's only a year and a half. He doesn't know."

"Thank goodness he doesn't know the truth about what happened. Do you think this whole experience will affect him in any way?" Harry asked the doctor.

"From what was reported, the woman didn't mistreat him. She did the best she could."

"She wasn't able to soothe him."

"They told us that he cried a lot," Harry added.

"The landlady said he cried the whole weekend," Adeline said.

"Poor baby, where is he now?" Angie asked.

"He's already asleep for the night. He was a little out of sorts today and didn't want to leave my side. He never took his nap this afternoon and fell asleep right after dinner."

"Were you able to go down to the police station?"

"Yes, this afternoon. I snuck out and left him with Harry and Sadie. Henry acted like he was angry with me when I returned."

"What did he do?"

"First, he pretended to ignore me and wouldn't come to me. After that, he clung to me for dear life and wouldn't let go of me for a second."

Dr. Abe reassured Adeline. "…And that's a perfectly normal reaction for a toddler, isn't it?"

"Yes, but it made me feel sad. I know I had to go to sign the papers and I wanted to see if I could speak to Penelope Gibbons."

"She's the lady that stole Henry."

"Yes, she was a *VAD* during the war. She reported directly to me. She's the one I sent home because she was pregnant. Do you remember the story I told you."

"Of course, how could I forget?"

"I wanted to apologize to her for my decision to immediately send her home during the war."

"Oh, Adeline, after what she did, she should be begging you for your forgiveness."

"I know, but somehow I felt sorry for her. I'm the one blessed with so much and she's all alone."

"What did she say when she saw you?"

"She was very apologetic. She said she wasn't thinking clearly. She thought she had made peace with the past. However she said that when she saw Henry in the baby carriage, she felt she wanted me to suffer the way she had suffered…

"I told her I was sorry that I didn't break the military rules and allow her to remain at the hospital camp for a few more weeks. I told her that her sergeant did come through Le Treport with the hospital convoy. She could have been with him. They could have spent a few more precious days together."

"It's all so sad."

"I told her that I often thought about her and prayed for her to this day. After the war I wrote to her but never received a return letter. Penelope said that when she learned Sergeant Kingsley had died, she felt too angry to write me. She was angry with her parents for not allowing her to go through with the pregnancy. She was angry with me for many years. You know, in a way, I don't blame her. Angie, she asked for my forgiveness."

"How can you forgive her, Adeline, after these past five miserable days?"

"I couldn't. It feels like she took more than my son from me. It feels like she robbed something deep inside of me. I hurt too much to forgive her, Angie. I know I should forgive but how do I begin to forgive her for what she did to me?"

"I can understand that. It will take time. Do you feel angry?"

"No, I think I feel sad more than anything. I feel sad that my decision hurt Penelope and she was forced to do what she did."

"It sounds like you've already taken the first step toward forgiveness."

"Why do you say that?" Adeline asked Angie.

"By putting yourself in her shoes, you are trying to understand the big picture of what happened."

"I am trying, Angie, but it's difficult. I have so much to be thankful for."

"Did you sign the police report?" Abe asked. "Will she stand trail and go to prison?"

"It was my intention to press charges against Penelope. That's the reason I went down to the station. I wanted her locked up for what she did to my family. When I arrived, I got an overwhelming urge to speak to her. I had to see her. I realized I needed to apologize to her for my part in the affair."

"What will happen to her?"

"You might think I'm foolish, but I didn't press charges. I couldn't cause her any more grief than what I already caused her. I asked

Detective O'Brien if they would let her go if I didn't sign the police statement."

"Can they just let her go free?" Abe asked.

"No, she's an immigrant who has now confessed to a crime. They will deport her."

"Oh, no, what will she do?"

"She told me she would be relieved to return home and put this behind her. She thought that it would be better if she went back to England because no one would know what she did. I asked her what she planned to do there. She said she'd get a job and save her money. She wants to open her own dress shop in London. Do you think she'll be okay, Angie?"

"Yes, I'm sure she will be and I'm certain you will, too."

Within a week the United States District Court for the Eastern District of New York convened on the case of Penelope Gibbons and ruled unanimously in favor of deportation. In the days before Penelope Gibbons returned to England, Adeline Steingold visited Penelope twice at the Metropolitan Women's Detention Center in Brooklyn. She was allowed to meet with her for thirty minutes in a windowless room on the third floor. During that time, Adeline searched deep inside herself to find a path toward forgiveness. On the morning Penelope sailed for Southampton, Adeline met her at the dock. As a gesture of her intention to forgive, Adeline placed an envelope in Penelope's hand. The envelope contained enough money to put a down payment on a dress shop in London.

Adeline stood on the dock and watched the ship as it was pulled out of the harbor by a tugboat. Satisfied that she had done the right thing, she headed home. That night, for the first time in months, she slept soundly and dreamt peacefully.

Chapter Thirty-Four

∼

November 1918
Stationary Hospital #16
Le Treport, France

The angels pray, the battles cease,
A treaty signed and there is peace.

The clouds darkened the sky and hovered above the hospital camp, lingering over the tents for hours. The branches on the acacia trees that surrounded base camp lay still and unmoving for not even the slightest breeze could be felt. Along with the massive cloud cover, came the quiet…a strange and eerie silence that traveled through the hospital camp making everyone anxious and uneasy. Everyone waited, silently anticipating a storm.

Always expecting another field ambulance convoy to arrive, the medics efficiently discharged the wounded and sent them on their way to *Blighty*. Still, they couldn't relax. They did their best to ready the camp, cleaning out the ward tents, rolling bandages and preparing cots for new admissions. While they waited, they restocked their cupboards with medicine, supplies and food rations. Each day they waited for a convoy to arrive but, hour after hour, none came.

With no news from the front, they wondered what was happening and why they weren't receiving casualties at their hospital. When there was nothing more to be done, the nursing superintendent granted the nurses a day's leave. Some hiked to the shore and walked in the gritty sand carved from the limestone cliffs. At the beach they could pretend there wasn't a war raging on the other side of France.

Others walked to the French village of Eu and enjoyed croissants with apple butter and fig jelly. Their omelets were cooked with the freshest eggs plucked that morning from under the hens in the chicken coop. In Eu, they learned that the Allies were advancing through France and would soon arrive at the German border. The optimistic villagers were confident that peace was coming for they heard talk that the Germans were ready to surrender and sign the treaty that had been prepared in Versailles months before. The nurses breathed a sigh of relief when they heard the encouraging news from the villagers.

Later as they finished up their supper, a deafening clap of thunder rattled the chairs they were sitting on. Some had grown so immune to the sounds of war that they didn't budge. Others jumped up from their seats and held their breaths, deciding if they should take cover inside or if there was time to run to base camp.

The decision was made almost immediately when they heard the call of the all-hands bugle.

They hurried back to camp to discover that a large convoy had arrived. This was one of the largest convoys by far, carrying triple the usual number of injured soldiers. They would need more cots and beds for the hundreds of wounded. Everyone pitched in, even the cooks and the camp pastor. Every medical officer, orderly, nurse and *VAD* helped to carry the wounded inside. As the unloading of the convoy was underway, the heavens opened and the downpour began, drenching everyone in an outburst of heavy torrential rain.

They needed more tents to protect the injured from the rain. As the nurses worked, cutting through boots, tearing uniforms, giving bed baths and dressing wounds, the orderlies prepared more tents. The recreation tent, the service tent, the mess tent and the nurses' tents were converted into hospital ward tents. In an hour's time, they had reorganized camp by assembling an additional row of pup tents for the nurses and *VAD*s along the perimeter of camp. In the next hour they transferred all of the nurses' belongings to the smaller tents.

During all the hectic activity of moving, the soldiers were upbeat and witty as the nurses worked through the long, rainy evening.

"It looks like we lost the battle, soldier."

The soldier laughed. "On the contrary, nurse, we were winning."

"Hate to see what you would look like if our side was losing, soldier," the nurse replied.

"You can be sure that *Fritz and Company* are in worst shape."

"The *jerries* retreated while we advanced."

"We didn't stop until we reached the border."

"Nurse, didn't you hear? The war will soon be over."

Adeline was called away to sit with a *D-I*, a young Brit who was suffering with gas gangrene toxemia.

The *M.O.* whispered, "Too late to amputate…doesn't have much time left…sepsis…sit with him, Sister, just 'til the end."

His medical record read: Chadwick Deverson, sev gsw, rt fem, gg. This meant severe gunshot wound in the right thigh bone with gas gangrene settling in. She sat down beside him. She heard the popping sounds of gas releasing from his infection. She knew that if she removed his bandage, she would find tissue necrosis and blisters oozing with pus.

"Am I dying, Sister?" he asked.

"You are severely wounded, Chadwick."

"They call me *Lankie*, you know, because I'm so tall. You can call me that, too."

"Where are you from, *Lankie*?"

"Hutton-Le-Hole."

"I'm afraid I don't know exactly where that is."

"North Yorkshire in the Ryeland, near Pickering, Miss…"

"Yes, I've heard of Pickering."

"A stream runs right through the middle of town. Promise me, Sister, to tell my sweetheart that I love her."

"What's her name?"

"Name's Laceyann."

"Can you give me her address?"

"Her address is right in there, in my *Sister Suzy Bag*. Please write to her."

"I promise, *Lankie*."

She held his hand and watched him as he closed his eyes. She saw his face relax and hoped it was peace that she witnessed, spreading across his face before he died.

Just then, the pup tent door flap flew open.

"The news is out! The *jerries* signed the armistice…means the war's soon over."

In a remote forest of Compiegne, the Germans had agreed to surrender all their heavy guns, machine guns, airplanes and submarines.

In addition, they revealed the location of all mines they had planted in the countryside and the many river springs they had poisoned. All fighting on the western front would cease on the eleventh hour on the eleventh day on the eleventh month, November, 11, 1918.

Chapter Thirty-Five

September 1926
New York City

At a celebration in the street
You never know whom you will meet.

"Mama, I don't even know Saint January. Why do I have to go?"

"Leonora, how is it that you do not know about him? He is the patron saint of Napoli. Didn't they teach you about the saints in school?"

"Yes, I thought we learned about all the saints but they never taught us about a Saint January."

Mrs. Bartoli looked toward the heavens and made the sign of the cross. "That's the American translation of his name. In Napoli, he is called San Gennaro. Is this the price we pay for leaving the old country?"

"Why do I have to go?" Leonora moaned.

"Because Papa is on the committee and he wants us both to be there beside him."

"Why would they even want to plan such an event?" Leonora asked.

"It's a celebration to honor the saint on his feast day. It's been a tradition in Napoli for centuries."

"Mama, this is America. You shouldn't be parading in the street like peasants. What will people think of us?"

"They will think that we are sharing our Italian traditions with the Americans."

Leonora asked. "Did Papa even get permission?"

"Yes, the committee members obtained permission from the alderman's office to close Mulberry Street for the parade."

"Why is it going to take all day?"

"Leonora, you ask too many questions. First we all go to Mass. Then they will have the procession through the street. The men will carry the statue out onto Mulberry Street and walk to the shrine they built. Then, noi mangiamo, we eat together."

"They built a shrine right there on Mulberry Street?"

"Yes, they built the shrine yesterday. It's all finished. Everything is all ready for tomorrow's celebration."

"I can see it now. By tomorrow morning the shrine will be covered with flowers and candles. Are we really going to eat on the pavement in the middle of the street?"

"I told you they are closing the street. Tomorrow morning, they will put out the tables and chairs and start setting up the grills."

"Mama, why can't we act like Americans?"

"Basta, Leonora. Abbastanza. Enough, it's just this one day. We do it for Papa. He doesn't ask much of us."

On September 19th Leonora and her parents arrived at Baxter Street and climbed the steps of The Church of The Most Precious

Blood to attend Mass. During Mass the priest told the story of San Gennaro, the martyred bishop of Benevento, who was imprisoned for his Christian beliefs during the reign of Emperor Diocletian in the fourth century. When he was sentenced to death and thrown to the wild bears in the Flavian Amphitheater in Naples, the bears refused to eat him. Emperor Diocletian eventually ordered the bishop to be beheaded. Shortly after San Gennaro died, a woman named Eusebia collected and saved his blood in two glass jars that were sealed. At the time this was a common practice. The blood clotted and dried out, but each year on the anniversary of the saint's beheading the blood lique-fies. To this day the people of Naples witness the miracle of the clot-ted blood liquefying at the cathedral on the feast day of San Gennaro, September 19th.

Leonora watched as the statue of San Gennaro was hoisted up onto the shoulders of six men after Mass. They carried the statue out of the church and lead the procession down Mulberry Street. A five-piece band of musicians followed directly behind them. As the solemn parade passed, people pinned offerings on the ribbons attached to the statue. Their donations would be saved to be distributed among the poor of the parish. Out on the street more speeches followed before the bless-ing of the food and pastries. Stomachs growled as the aroma of grilled onions and peppers and the fried dough of the zeppole filled the air.

It was only after they had eaten a hearty lunch and the espresso and zeppole were being served, that Leonora spotted Alfonso and his family. She wanted to sink under the table and disappear. Instead she turned to watch the dancers dancing in the street and pretended not to notice them. However her Papa, in a rare jovial mood, called out a greeting to Mr. Ferrara.

"Oh no," Leonora groaned as she slide down in her chair.

Mr. Ferrara walked over to the table with his son Alfonso. "Good afternoon, Mr. Bartoli and Mrs. Bartoli, how are you this wonderful day?"

Alfonso bowed and said. "Good afternoon, Leonora."

Leonora was speechless. She smiled but couldn't say a word.

"Fine, fine, are you enjoying the feast?" Mr. Bartoli asked.

"Yes, Eugenio, I'm told you are one of the committee members who organized the festivities. It's turned out to be a fine celebration."

"I'm glad it's a success. Everyone appears to be enjoying themselves this afternoon."

"I must thank you for your efforts. Does the committee have plans to hold a festival again next year?"

"If all goes well, perhaps our feast will become a New York tradition."

"I hope so."

"May I ask who this handsome young man is, Mr. Ferrara?"

"Eugenio, you remember my son, Alfonso."

"Of course, he has grown into a fine looking fellow," Mr. Bartoli commented as he studied the young man. "I remember when you were a youngster helping your papa in his shop. Do you work with your father now?"

"No, I'm afraid I am not following in my father's footsteps," Alfonso answered.

"He is going to be an attorney next year," Mr. Ferrara announced proudly. "He already has an offer for a position at a fancy firm on Madison Avenue."

"Ah, such is the blessing of being in America," Mrs. Bartoli said.

"Alfonso, where are you going to law school?" Mr. Bartoli asked.

"I graduated City College two years ago and am now attending St. John's Law School."

"That's very impressive. The years are passing so quickly. You have already graduated from college and are now in law school." Mr. Bartoli turned to Mr. Ferrara and said, "You must be very proud of your son."

"Yes, we are!"

"Where are my manners? Would either of you like a cannoli?" Mrs. Bartoli offered both men the pastry dish.

"No, I've already eaten my fair share of pastries today," Mr. Ferrara said as he rubbed his belly. "We are on our way home. That is, after I find my wife. She was here a moment ago and now she's disappeared into the crowd."

"I hope your evening is as pleasant as the afternoon has been," Alfonso said. Then looking directly at Leonora, he bowed. "Good evening, Leonora," he said as he left.

Leonora nodded and politely smiled.

After Alfonso and his father left the table, Eugenio Bartoli scolded his daughter. "Couldn't you say hello and be polite-a? Why you not say a word? You embarrass your papa. I ask-a you, you want-a them to think I have a rude daughter?"

"No, Papa, it's just…"

"It's just that you don't want-a get married, I know. I know. I heard-a this many times before. You're not interested in meeting handsome young men who are going to be rich attorneys. He turned to his wife. "Mama, you should tell your daughter that she's-a not getting any younger."

"Next time, Papa, I will. I promise you," Leonora said, apologetically.

"Listen, Mama, I have an idea. How about we invite the Ferraras for dinner next Sunday? You make-a the sauce and the pasta. I buy-a the cannoli."

"That would be nice, Eugenio. I would like to invite them," Mama replied.

"Yes, the whole family. You invite them and maybe Leonora could try to be nice-a to that young man. What-a was his name?"

"Alfonso, Papa."

"Yes, the young man, Alfonso, who is going to be a rich attorney on Madison Avenue. Leonora, do you think you can-a be nice to him for one day when he comes on Sunday?"

"Yes, Papa, if that's what you want. I can be very nice to Mr. Ferrara's son on Sunday, as nice and polite as I can be."

"Good, now that's-a my girl. It's time you started to listen to your Papa."

Try as she might, Leonora could not contain her smile.

Chapter Thirty-Six

September 1926
New York City

Ever so grateful that all is well,
The past is not a place to dwell.

The settlement house on Henry Street was not one house as its name implies, but a series of attached brick townhouses which, over the years, had been generously donated to the Visiting Nurses Association. The buildings were connected in the rear by a tranquil garden park and a children's playground. The playground was one of the first of its kind to be built within the limits of the crowded city. New York City planners were now using the Henry Street playground as a model for public playground projects currently planned for the children living within the city.

Adeline found Lillian Wald on her knees in the garden, planting fall tulip bulbs which would be ready to bloom in the spring.

"How are you, Adeline? What do I owe the pleasure of your visit today?" Miss Wald asked as she stood up.

"I wanted to come down and personally thank you for what you did to help me and my family. I intended to visit you earlier, but there was so much going on with the kidnapping and the police investigation."

"I didn't expect a personal visit. I received your letter two weeks ago and that was more than sufficient. Your thank-you note was heartwarming and beautifully written." Lillian quickly rinsed off her hands in a nearby pail of water. "Come. Let's sit in the gazebo and talk." As she dried her hands on her cotton apron, she asked, "May I offer you a cup of tea?"

"No, thank you, it's enough for me just to sit in this tranquil setting. Your garden and gazebo are lovely."

"They aren't mine. They belong to the local community that designed and built the garden and gazebo. You would have been amazed to see so many neighbors working together on this project. A group of volunteers still come regularly to tend to the garden. It was built for them, you know, so that families would have a quiet, relaxing place in this busy city. But, enough about Henry Street, what can I do for you today, my dear?"

"Nothing, Miss Wald, you've done so much already. I came down to thank you for allowing your nurses to search for my son."

"No thank you is necessary, Adeline. Please call me, Lillian."

"Certainly, I came to thank you, Lillian."

"We were only doing our part to help one of our own."

"Above and beyond your part, I feel."

"It's the others you should thank."

"Yes, that's what I had in mind. I would like to do something for Henry House and the nurses. Are you in need of funds for a special project that you would like to start?"

"Fortunately, we are continuing to operate in the black. However I am on the committee to increase the number of public playgrounds for the children in the city."

"Yes, we heard. I'm pleased to tell you that the Steingold Foundation has allotted a sizeable amount of funds to donate to the project at the end of the year."

"That is wonderful to hear, Adeline. Thank you."

"Is there anything we can do specifically for the Henry Street nurses?"

"Right now, our biggest challenge is recruiting nurses. There aren't enough trained nurses for all the work that needs to be done. The demand is great and our nurses are terribly overworked."

"Maybe I can assist in your efforts in some way."

"Henry Street has developed a task force for recruitment. You might like to meet with the group and lend them your ideas."

"I'd like that. I would also like to host a thank-you lunch or dinner to show my gratitude to your visiting nurses."

"How can I refuse such a proposal? Perhaps you could host a party during the holidays."

"I was thinking sooner, maybe sometime later this month?"

"I think the nurses would like that very much. On behalf of the deserving women I work with, I accept your offer. I'm certain the nurses would enjoy a special dinner in their honor. What do you have in mind?"

At the end of September, Adeline and Harry Steingold hosted a catered affair in the main ballroom of the Waldorf Astoria Hotel for the visiting nurses of Henry Street and the volunteers of Nativity House. They hired popular band leader Vincent Lopez and his orchestra to entertain that evening. A dozen tables were lavishly decorated with white roses and candles that had been painted navy blue and silver. The special dinner began with a jumbo shrimp cocktail appetizer followed by a choice of Lobster Thermidor, Beef Wellington or Roasted Rack of Lamb as an entree. The honored guests were delighted with a presentation of dramatic desserts of both Crepe Suzettes and Cherries Jubilee after dinner.

Adeline and Harry Steingold gave a thank-you speech, praising the nurses for their selfless spirit, charitable enthusiasm and willingness to volunteer when they were asked to join the search for Henry. Afterward Adeline called forth each nurse by name and presented her with a gift of a fourteen-carat gold angel pin which Harry had specially designed for the occasion. On the back of every pin was this inscription: *The Steingold Family remains forever grateful to our guardian angels.*

Adeline announced that the Steingold Foundation was in the process of establishing a scholarship for young women interested in studying the field of nursing. The foundation would pay their nursing school tuition if they agreed to work as Henry Street visiting nurses after graduation. Miss Wald was overjoyed with the Steingolds' generous program which would make a significant impact on her efforts to recruit visiting nurses to her organization.

The Steingolds hired the hotel photographer to take pictures throughout the evening. However when the photographer approached Harry and Adeline for a family photograph, they declined.

The week before Adeline wouldn't allow her family to be photographed at the wedding of Maureen O'Shaughnessy and Samuel Goodwin. After the wedding ceremony, their wedding reception was a joyous affair held in the Henry Street gardens on a sunny Saturday afternoon in September. Maureen's family and nursing colleagues from both Henry Street and Nativity House were invited. Harry and Adeline brought their children, Sadie and Henry, to the party. Everyone was in a celebratory mood as they danced and sang into the early evening. The happy groom had hired a professional photographer to take pictures throughout the afternoon's festivities. The photographer took lovely photographs of the beautiful bride and her handsome groom, as well as the wedding party and guests, in and around the white gazebo in the garden. However when the photographer approached Harry and Adeline for permission to shoot a family photograph, they refused to pose.

"No pictures, please," Harry and Adeline said in unison. They looked at Angie and smiled. Adeline shrugged her shoulders and laughed. "We learned our lesson this year the hard way. We're going to be extra cautious about photographing the children until they are older."

Chapter Thirty-Seven

♋

October 1926
Home,
Brooklyn, New York

A home becomes a scared place
Where love forever grows.

Even though the house on Bushwick Avenue was smaller than many of the other houses that lined that avenue, it was still considered a mansion. It wasn't the thirteen rooms that attracted Harry Steingold to the property; it was the private, hedge-lined, wrought-iron fence that surrounded the house. When he showed the house to his wife, they both immediately agreed that it was the perfect home for their growing family.

The sale of the house to the Steingolds took less than a month. Having rented an apartment at the Waldorf Astoria for so long, they had little furniture, but Harry and Adeline moved into their new home anyway. The Steingolds arrived just as autumn leaves were beginning to drop onto their front lawn. Adeline decided to decorate the children's rooms first. She had already hired an artist to paint a mural for Sadie's room. When Sadie announced that she wanted to go to sleep with six angels surrounding her bed, the artist painted them to her satisfaction. When the mural was completed, Sadie was thrilled.

Adeline asked Sadie to help her choose a theme for Henry's room. They decided on baby barnyard animals. The artist was inspired by their idea and quickly produced a number of pencil sketches for them to see.

As Adeline sat in Henry's room rocking him, she tried to imagine the placement of the baby animals on the walls. Even after he was fast asleep in her arms, Adeline couldn't put Henry down in his crib. She continued to rock him, enjoying the warm weight of his little body on her chest. The scent of Ivory soap and baby powder filled the air around her with baby sweetness. Taking a deep breath, she savored the smell of the toddler's chunky hands and sweaty head. She always enjoyed this time of night, singing to him after giving him a bath, powdering him and struggling to get him into his blue long-john pajamas. Her heart overflowed with gratitude and love for the boy as she gently rocked him in her rocking chair. Adeline softly hummed a lullaby until her eyelids grew heavy and her sleepy eyes closed.

Even though the Armistice had been signed on November 11, 1918, it still took over a year to dismantle the base camp hospitals in western France. Adeline remained in Le Treport until the last remaining British *VAD* was safely on the train to Calais and heading toward the ferry to Dover, England. Once all her nurses and *VAD*s were accounted for, Adeline faced a myriad of additional administrative assignments before she could even think about sailing home. She began the work of processing reports and dismantling hospitals.

From Le Treport, Adeline was transferred to Wimerex, Boulogne and then to the large hospital in Etaples. Weeks turned into months as the nurses waited for the last of the injured soldiers to regain their health and strength so that they would be well enough to travel. Only then did they pack up and leave for home. Adeline finally arrived at the port of Southampton, England with her commanding officer in late November 1919. They joined the last convoy of army nurses returning to the United States. No one saw them off as they boarded the military hospital ship. Unlike the morning they had arrived three years before, there was no farewell band or celebratory fanfare on the pier that day. The war had been over for more than a year. The people in England had already begun the work of putting the war behind them as they returned to their pre-war lives. Adeline thought of the thousands of lives which would remain forever altered by the war. There were so many who would carry on forever with the memory of lost lives, lost loves and lost limbs.

The ship's final destination was The Walter Reed National Military Hospital in Maryland but first the ship stopped at Ellis Island in New York Harbor. There they were to pick up any remaining injured soldiers recuperating at Ellis Island and transfer them to the hospital in Maryland. Adeline planned to disembark at Ellis Island and eventually take the train to Connecticut from New York City. She hoped to spend the holidays with her family before returning to her former position at Ellis Island Hospital.

With no assignment other than to complete her reports, Adeline relaxed while onboard. She did not mind the gusty winds and high waves. In fact, the rhythmic movement of the ship allowed her to sleep soundly. Sleep was an escape from the sounds of artillery that still rang in her ear. For the short time while she slept, she dreamt of home. In France during the war, Adeline often wondered if she would ever return to the States or if she would ever see her home again. She often thought about Harry, a love she had given up when she volunteered to serve as a military nurse.

The gusty winds at sea helped the ship arrive in the port of New York two days earlier than scheduled. As the Statue of Liberty looked down upon her when the steamship passed, Adeline said a prayer of gratitude. She was surprised and delighted to see Sister Gwendolyn Hanover, the Superintendant of Nurses at Ellis Island Hospital, waiting at the ferry landing to greet Adeline.

Sister welcomed her with open arms. "It's wonderful to finally see you. I've waited so long for your return."

"Thank you, Sister. Have the others returned?"

"All our nurses are accounted for. They are slowly returning one by one. When are you planning to return to your position here at Ellis Island Hospital? We have your old room at the Nurses' Cottage clean and ready for you to move in."

"I have a number of military reports to complete. Then I want to spend some time with my cousins in Connecticut. I should like to start back at the end of January. Does than fit your staffing needs?"

"It will have to. You must take a well-deserved rest before you begin your work here at the hospital."

"Yes, Sister, thank you."

"I will admit that we're very short of staff now that the war is over and immigration from Europe has begun once again. I've posted notices and we're hiring new nursing staff." Sister Hanover frowned. "Sadly, some of you didn't return," she said.

"Mary's gone."

"I know, dear, I was broken-hearted when I received the news. We lost five in all.

"They all died of influenza during the epidemic."

"We will miss them terribly. They gave the ultimate sacrifice for the boys and their country."

"Oh, Sister, it was terrible to lose them."

"I know, dear," Sister put her arm around Adeline as she escorted her to the ferry that was going to New York City. At the ferry ramp, she looked at her and gave her a kiss on each cheek. "You best be on your way now so that you can return to us soon. Rest assured that you're home, dear, you're safe. There's nothing to worry about. We have you back in our arms. You're home, now and forever."

Harry slowly opened the door to the nursery and peeked in.

"Is Henry asleep?" he whispered.

"Shhh, yes…"

"Don't you want to put him down in his crib?"

"Just a few more minutes," Adeline said.

"Don't be too long, darling, you need your rest. I have a cozy fire started in our bedroom."

"Yes, dear, I'll meet you there."

Harry stood at the door, studying his wife as she continued to softly hum to the sleeping child. Then he quietly closed the door and smiled.

Adeline kissed the top of the child's head and whispered, "Good night, my sweet. You're home, dear, you're safe. There's nothing to worry about. We have you back in our arms. You're home, now and forever."

THE END

Author's Notes

Tell your story with truth and tact, or Fact
Becomes Fiction and Fiction becomes Fact!

Angels in Brooklyn is a work of fiction presented in a historical setting. History forms the framework for historical fiction. From there a story is created around historical events. Historical fiction has the potential to be a fascinating teaching tool but it carries the potential of compromising real-life events, by sometimes enhancing and sometimes distorting history.

Some of the people, places and events in this novel are real and are not a product of my imagination. Here are some historical facts that influenced my writing.

Businesses in the 1920s

<u>Rexall Pharmacies</u>: In 1902 Louis Liggett united 40 privately owned drug stores into a Rexall cooperative.

<u>The Bartoli Shoe Store</u>: It was established in 1890 by Eugenio Bartoli, my husband's grandfather. He sold high-quality, hand-crafted shoes on Manhattan's Upper East Side.

<u>The Waldorf-Astoria Hotel</u>: The original Waldorf Hotel in New York City was built by William Waldorf Astor in 1893. It became the grandest hotel in the world after William Astor collaborated with his cousin, John Astor, to open The Waldorf-Astoria Hotel.

ANGELS IN BROOKLYN

Ellis Island Hospital

Ellis Island Hospital closed its doors over sixty years ago, but the buildings still stand on the island. The general hospital opened in 1902 and the contagious disease hospital in 1911. When you come to New York or New Jersey, don't miss a visit to the Statue of Liberty and Ellis Island Monument operated by the National Park Service. For the cost of the boat ride, you can visit both Ellis Island and Liberty Island. Before docking at the pier of the Ellis Island Immigrant Museum, the ferry passes the southernmost part of the island. You can see the buildings that once housed the 450-bed contagious disease hospital and the magnificent structure that was home to the 275-bed general hospital. The non-profit *Save Ellis Island Foundation* was established to increase public awareness and funding to preserve the hospital complex as a future educational conference center.

(www.saveellisisland.org)

Feast of San Gennaro

The celebration of the beloved Italian saint, San Gennaro, started on Mulberry Street in Little Italy, New York in 1926. It was a one-day festival to honor the saint on his feast day, September 19th. Today the Feast of San Gennaro is a popular, annual, New York tradition held during the month of September which usually lasts eleven days.

Helen Dore Boylston

Helen Dore Boylston (April 4, 1895 - September 30, 1984) is the author of the *Sue Barton* novels and the *Carol Page* series. She published a diary of her memoirs as a World War One nurse entitled *Sister: The War*

Diary of a World War I Nurse (3). The events that Helen Dore Boylston writes about in a letter to Adeline in Chapter Sixteen were based on her memoirs (3).

Lillian Wald

Lillian Wald (March 10, 1867 – September 1, 1940) was an innovative nurse leader and the founder of Henry Street Settlement House. She is the author of *The House on Henry Street* (17), which records the history of her settlement house and the beginning of The Visiting Nurse Service of New York. Today the Henry Street Settlement House remains open as a vital community resource.

(www.henrystreet.org)

Mansions on Bushwick Avenue

There are a number of elaborate mansions still standing on Bushwick Avenue in Brooklyn, New York. Many of these homes were built by German brewery owners who established their breweries and beerhouses in Brooklyn in the late 1800. Later the avenue became known as *Doctor's Row* when these mansions became the homes of doctors, bankers and New York businessmen.

The Statue of Liberty

The Statue of Liberty has been standing on Liberty Island in New York harbor since it was dedicated in October 1886. The structure was designed by the noted French sculptor, Frederic Bartholdi. Called *Liberty Enlightening the World*, it was offered as a gift from France to the United States and remains a symbol of democracy.

(www.statueofliberty.org)

ANGELS IN BROOKLYN

World War One

The First World War began on July 28, 1914. At the time World War One was called *The Great War* or *The War to End All Wars*. It was inconceivable that another world war would follow less than 30 years later. The Allies fought against the Central Powers for three years before the United States entered the war in 1917. The Armistice of November 11, 1918 (also known as the Armistice of Compiegne) marked the end of World War One on the eleventh hour of the eleventh day of the eleventh month in 1918.

World War One Nursing Stories

The *Casualty Evacuation Chain* snaked through France from the *Dressing Stations* nearest the front to the Port of Calais. Historians can find ample documentation of its many hospital stops along the way and thus trace the route that the wounded soldiers took to return to England. At the time of the signing of the Armistice on November 11, 1918, it was reported that of the 10,000 nurses and aides stationed in Europe during the war, almost 500 died as a result of meningitis, pneumonia, influenza and tuberculosis. Adeline's many nursing memories were taken from the diaries of these heroic World War One nurses and *VAD*s who served in Europe during the First World War: Vera Brittain (2), Helen Dore Boylston (3), Dorothea Crewdson (7), Olive Dent (8) and Shirley Millard (13).

Acknowledgments

Thanks to the technology of the internet and electronic readers, like Kindle and Nook, the diaries of British, Australian, and American nurses and *VAD*s who served in World War One became accessible a few years ago. After re-reading Helen Dore Boylston's novel, *Sue Barton, Student Nurse* (4), I remembered Boylston had written a diary of her experiences as a nurse during World War One. Her published diary was not accessible to me until the kindle edition of *Sister: The War Diary of a World War I Nurse* (3) was published by Uncommon Valor Press in 2015.

Despite tremendous wartime challenges, Helen's diary is filled with lively stories. Her cheerful, upbeat nature penetrates her writing. She possesses all the resilience and determination of her fictional character, *Sue Barton*, which she created years later in 1936. The diary has an interesting ending: "Kit says there is a lot happening in the Balkans and she thinks she may join the Red Cross and go. Would I come with her? Would I? Daddy wants me to settle down ... but I'm young. I'm young. What is old age to me if it has no memories? Kitty and I sail on the New Amsterdam tomorrow for Paris! The world in mine!!" (3) Helen wasn't ready to settle down at home after the war so she joined the Red Cross and served in the war-ravaged Balkans.

During a train ride Helen Boylston met Rose Ingalls, a journalist. It was Rose Ingalls who influenced and encouraged both Helen and Rose's mother, Laura Ingalls, (*Little House on the Prairie*) to publish their diaries.

ANGELS IN BROOKLYN

After reading *Sister: The War Diary of a World War I Nurse*, I spent the next summer reading the diaries of other World War One nurses and *VAD*s. I was amazed by the endurance of these dedicated young ladies and awed by both their selfless spirit and willingness to sacrifice for their country. Throughout all the hardships they suffered, they kept their spirits high and amused themselves with parties, shows, and minor flirtations.

Reading the diaries of English and Australian nurses proved to be a challenge. I continually referred to the dictionary and the terminology sections in order to translate the English of a hundred years ago into today's English. I was inspired to write about Adeline's wartime experiences because I wanted to translate these nursing stories for today's nurse.

I started my nursing career in 1968 and had the opportunity to experience nursing before electronic technology – two different types of nursing. Today's nursing is different from yesterday's but the heart of nursing remains the same. Although they're not camping out in the frozen wilderness, nurses continue to work through the night when the rest of us are sound asleep and face the cold at five in the morning to prepare for their early morning shifts. Today's resilient nurses are just as courageous as yesterday's nurses as they fearlessly face every challenge that is put before them.

I am sending special thanks to my editor and friend, Cathy Lavin, who teaches as she edits, offers inspiration and keeps my spirits high. I am most appreciative of my son Albert Limata who also edits my work as he is a gifted writer. My husband Al and my sister, Dr. Patricia Ann Marcellino, are my indispensable sounding boards and always my first readers.

I thank both Frank Marcellino and Marilyn Marcellino. Frank is a master at coming up with innovative and descriptive covers for the novels in the Ellis Angels series. Marilyn's youthful face is the model for the covers of all the Ellis Angels novels.

Thank you to my long-time nurse friends, Terry Campisi, Elaine Eastman, Jennifer O'Keefe and Judith Sanderson, who have encouraged me to keep writing.

A special thank you goes out to the many new nurse friends I've made since I began writing historical fiction. I truly appreciate how you took time out of your busy schedules to write to me and review my novels.

Resources

(1) ANON, *A War Nurse Diary: Sketches from a Belgian Field Hospital*, London: Diggory Press, 2005 and Pickle Partner Publishing, 2014.

(2) Bostridge, Mark, *Vera Brittain and the First World War: The Story of Testament of Youth*, London: Bloomsbury Publications, 1933.

(3) Boylston, Helen Dore, *Sister: The War Diary of a Nurse*, New York: Ives Washburn Publisher, 1927 and Uncommon Valor Publishers, 2015.

(4) Boylston, Helen Dore, *Sue Barton: Student Nurse*, New York: Little, Brown & Company, 1936.

(5) Butler, Janet, *Kitty's War: The Remarkable Wartime Experiences of Kit*, Queensland: University of Queensland Press, 2013.

(6) Colley, Rupert, *World War One: History in an Hour*, London: Harper Press, 2012.

(7) Crewdson, Richard, *Dorothea's War: A First World War Nurse Tells Her Story*, Great Britain: Weidenfeld and Nicolson, 2013.

(8) Dent, Olive, *A Volunteer Nurse on the Western Front*, London: Random House Publishers, 1917.

(9) De Vries, Susanna, *Australian Heroines of World War One*, Australia: Piros Press, 2013.

(10) Hallett, Christine, *Veiled Warriors: Allied Nurses of the First World War*, Oxford: Oxford Press, 2014.

(11) Harris, Kirsty, *More than Bombs and Bandages: Australian Army Nurses at Work in World War I*, Australia: Big Sky Publishing, 2011.

(12) Mayhew, Emily, *Wounded: A New History of the Western Front in World War One*, Oxford: Oxford Press, 2013.

(13) Millard, Shirley, *I Saw Them Die: Diary and Recollections of Shirley Millard*, New York: Harcourt Brace - Journeys and Memoirs Series, 1936.

(14) Powell, Anne, *Women in the War Zone: Hospital Service in the First World War*, Great Britain: The History Press, 2013.

(15) Rees, Peter, *Anzacs Girls: The Extraordinary Story of our World War I Nurses*, Australia/New Zealand: Allen and Unwin, 2008.

(16) Smith, Betty, *A Tree Grows in Brooklyn*, New York: Harper Collins Publishers Inc, 1943.

(17) Wald, Lillian D., *The House on Henry Street*, New York: Forgotten Books, 2012 (Originally published by Henry Holt and Company, 1915).

About the Author

Carole Lee Limata graduated with an Associate Degree in Nursing from Queens College in 1968. After taking her Nursing Boards that summer, she worked as a registered nurse at New York City's Metropolitan Hospital and then at the City's Premature Nursery Center located at Elmhurst Hospital before moving to Northern California. She received a Bachelor's Degree in Nursing from Sacramento State University and earned a Master's Degree in Nursing from the University of California at San Francisco in 1980.

Carole's forty-year nursing career began as a staff nurse. She advanced to supervisor, maternity faculty member and prenatal educator before becoming a Director of a Maternity Department. She retired from her final position as supervisor of the screening programs at the Kaiser Permanente Genetics Department in Oakland, California in 2008.

In 2017, Carole received an Excellence in Nursing Research Award from Sigma Theta Tau International, Nu Xi chapter (The International Nurses' Honor Society) in recognition of her novels about nursing history .

When she is not writing, Carole's family keeps her busy. She enjoys her time with her loving husband, three wonderful grown children, two terrific sons-in-law and four beautiful grandchildren.

Discussion Guide

1. The novel begins when Adeline dreams about her experiences during World War One. Some of her dreams distort reality. When she is awake, she explains how she remembers the events. Do you remember your dreams when you wake up? Did you ever keep a dream journal? Do you agree with Harry when he encouraged Adeline to bring her dreams into the light of day? (Chapter 1)

2. Adeline talks of a mother's worry concerning the possibility of her son's future military service. She says, "It's every mother's worry, I suppose. There's nothing any of us can do about it." Do you agree with that statement? Have you ever had a close friend or family member in the military during wartime? (Chapter 2)

3. The settlement house played an important role in shaping a diverse community. How did it influence the lives of the immigrants? What impact did it have on the Americanization of immigrants? (Chapter 3)

4. Abe and Angie were not offended when the Steingolds were featured prominently on the front page cover of the newspaper. Would you have felt hurt if the same thing had happened to you? On the other hand, Adeline was very upset. Do you agree with her husband's suggestion for a future article? (Chapter 4)

5. Dr. Abe orders hydrogen peroxide and heat as a treatment for an ear infection before antibiotics were available. Many old world treatments were highly effective. Do you know of any? Do you

know of other treatments used to treat ear infections before anti-biotics? (Chapter 8)

6. Do you believe that Adeline made the correct decision to send *VAD* Penelope Gibbons back home to England when she learned Penelope was pregnant? Would you have bent the rules when Penelope asked to stay at base camp? (Chapter 11)

7. We now have more information about the causes of *SIDS* (sudden infant death syndrome). Was Dr. Abe on the right track when he suggested documenting patient histories? Did you note that the O'Donegal baby was sleeping on his stomach in the baby carriage? (Chapter 13)

8. Do the math on the Rouen hospital report to gain an additional perspective on how difficult and intense the work was. The hospital reported they did 935 surgeries and treated 4,853 patients in ten days. (Chapter 16)

9. Leonora Bartoli keeps her relationship with Alfonso a secret for over a year. Do you think Leonora should have told her parents or at least her mother about her boyfriend? (Chapter 19)

10. When asked if they would be interested in enrolling their children in the afterschool programs and summer school, both Mrs. Moratelli and Mrs. Tatjana want to think about it. Why are the immigrants reluctant to sign-up for the settlement house programs? (Chapter 18 and Chapter 20)

11. Why is Mrs. Tatjana avoiding questions from outsiders? Why is she not letting anyone in or out of the family system? Why was she hesitant to enroll the girls in school? Why didn't she answer the door to admit the visiting nurse to her home? Do you think she was embarrassed because her husband left her? Do you think

she felt guilty because she was leaving her girls without adult supervision? (Chapter 20)

12. What do you think about the Tatjana girls being left alone all day and into the evening? Do you think Dr. Abe is correct in planning to report Mrs. Tatjana if she didn't enroll the girls in school? (Chapter 20)

13. Did you ever have to care for a younger sibling? Did you resent it/enjoy it? Was it a burden? What was it like to have the responsibility of a younger brother or sister? (Chapter 21)

14. Adeline and Harry appear to not blame their nurse, Rachel Zinzer, for leaving baby Henry unattended. Do you think it is unusual that they trust her? Is she responsible for the child's disappearance? Should they have fired her? (Chapter 26)

15. The nurses felt that the immigrants trusted the nurses over the police and men in uniform. Do you think that sentiment is the same for today's immigrant population? (Chapter 27 and Chapter 29)

LUNA BABIES

A Story of the Incubator Babies Exhibit
At Luna Park, Coney Island, New York

A Novel by Carole Lee Limata, RN, MSN

"When you first hear the barker's call beckoning you to view the tiny babies inside, you wonder what oddities of nature you will see at the Infant Incubator Exhibit at Luna Park. Intrigued, you pull a dime from your waistcoat pocket to pay the admission fee and soon find you are in a hospital-like setting. Your heart goes out to the helpless premature infants, growing in their man-made incubators, cared for by the tender hands of their nurses..." (Excerpt from *Luna Babies*)

Luna Babies is a story of the popular premature baby exhibit that existed for forty years at one of Coney Island's largest amusement parks, Luna Park. From 1903 to 1943, 8,000 premature infants were cared for by Dr. Walther Baier and displayed to spectators who paid admission to view them. This is the story of Dr. Walther Baier and his family, chronicled through the narratives of the doctor, his wife, his daughter and his nurse. Was Dr. Baier showcasing the premature babies as freaks of nature, exploiting them for his own financial gain or was he providing them with the highest level of healthcare which was their only hope for survival?

Here's the first chapter...

LUNA BABIES

1943

In the midst of a looming storm, the sky darkened and the ocean groaned. White-capped breakers crashed against the shore, devouring the grainy beach below the boardwalk. Overhead, a flock of seagulls flew inland. Eva hurried along the promenade, eager to reach the exhibit before the downpour started.

Her father's Infant Incubator Exhibit was located in the heart of Coney Island's Luna Park. The playground was closed, like it was every winter. Boarded-up attractions on the deserted midway stood frozen in suspension, hibernating until the next summer season. Eva passed closed vendor shacks as her footsteps echoed on the weathered wood, the only sounds to be heard through the park. At her feet, paper wrappers twirled in the crisp breeze on the sandy planks.

Earlier in the day, her father had left their Sea Gate home, a mile away, to say his final goodbye. When dusk approached and he hadn't returned, Eva began to worry. She left the house hurriedly, forgetting the key to the exhibit building. As she rushed along the midway, she wondered if she would find the entrance door locked.

Eva felt a flush of relief when she reached the exhibit and put her hand on the doorknob. It tuned easily and the front door creaked open.

"Papa! Papa!" Eva called, running through the nursery rooms.

In the dark, Eva reached for the electric light button but quickly remembered that the electricity had been turned off the day before. Adjusting her eyes, she fumbled to find the staircase and slowly walked up to the second floor. When she reached the landing, a feeling of dread overcame her. She braced herself for whatever she might find. She tread cautiously then, taking measured steps, carefully checking every bedroom before making her way back down the stairs.

She called out once more.

"Papa! Papa! Papa!"

In answer to her call, her echo resonated through the empty rooms.

And then...a faint whisper...

"In here, *Liebling*, I'm in here."

Eva rushed into the lecture hall, relieved to find her father sitting in a front-row seat.

He did not turn upon her approach but sat in deep reverie.

Finally, he spoke.

"Remember how Madame Jacquelyn would lecture to the crowds?" He asked. "They listened so attentively, and when we brought in the babies..."

"Oh, yes, Papa, when we brought in the babies dressed in their little caps and booties, how the audience *oohed* and *aahed* in amazement."

"We did good work, you know, but some...they never did understand."

"It's over now. They've taken everything away."

"The men came yesterday. They took the incubators off the walls and carried them out." He whispered.

"We're closed. Rest assured, Papa, your work here is finished."

"Yes, dear, my work is done."

"Papa, a storm is brewing." Eva looked concerned. "It's time to leave."

Eva helped her father out of the chair. She took hold of his arm as they walked through to the front rooms of the exhibit.

"Wait, Eva, wait. I promised Mr. Arlington that I would put up the notice before I left today."

"I'll do it, Papa."

Eva escorted her father out of the building and locked the door behind her. She placed a hand-written sign on the doorknob. As she left the exhibit, she looked back through the drizzle of rain. On the sign, three words had been printed boldly in black ink.

<u>**EXHIBIT**</u>

<u>**PERMANENTLY**</u>

<u>**CLOSED**</u>

Chapter One

Eva Baier
New York

Until I was seven years old, I lived with my mother and father in their apartment suite on the second floor of the Infant Incubator Exhibit at Coney Island. My father's Luna Park exhibit showcased growing premature infants in their incubators to the paying public during the busy summer seasons.

In the springtime when the babies began to arrive, the nurses moved in and lived with us. Two nurses were assigned to an apartment with a shared bathroom. Six apartments accommodated a dozen, trained, professional nurses on the second floor. Emelie, our cook, and Madame Jacquelyn Dominique, the Nursing Supervisor, also lived with us. Each had her own private apartment on the ground floor.

Mama began her spring cleaning in April, starting at the top of the building and scrubbing down to the bottom of the basement. She scoured and polished, washed and waxed, dusted and fluffed. With Emelie trailing behind and following all of Mama's directives, the entire exhibit building was spotlessly clean in a matter of weeks. When Mama was finished, the house sparkled. Mama would take off her apron and hang it up on the hook in the kitchen. Then she would proudly announce to Papa, "Doctor, your exhibit is now open for business!"

ANGELS IN BROOKLYN

It was always exciting when the nurses were in the process of moving in. In those days, the same nurses returned year after year. I got to know them and I had my favorites. They instructed me to politely knock when I wanted to visit with them in their bedrooms. If I did this correctly, they would open their doors and grant me entrance. I liked to sit on their beds and listen to them, laughing and talking to each other. They giggled and spoke of their adventures and their beaus.

In the summertime when the exhibit was open, I was only allowed to wander through the hallways in the evening after dinner. During the day, I had to be very, very quiet because the night nurses were sleeping. I often went barefoot. When the nurses were downstairs working in the nursery, they never joked. They were very serious and professional, but upstairs they relaxed. We all had a good time.

In addition to the nurses' quarters, there were two sleeping rooms for the wet nurses who were employed at the Infant Incubator Exhibit. A "wet nurse" is a ridiculously silly name for a woman who is paid to share her breastmilk with babies who are not her own. Papa paid them handsomely for their lactating service. They often lived nearby and traveled to and from the nursery because they had babies and toddlers waiting for them at home. They each worked three, twelve-hour shifts per week. Papa would never allow them to work more than that in one week. He insisted that they get plenty of rest and sleep. For this reason, they were allowed to nap in the sleeping rooms between feedings. He encouraged them to maintain a daily regimen of hourly hydration and pristine hygiene. Fresh air and exercise were always on the schedule.

After Emelie served a nutritious breakfast, the wet nurses would begin feeding the babies who were strong enough to breastfeed. After the feedings, the wet nurses were encouraged to take a morning walk on Surf Avenue to breathe in the ocean air. Upon returning, Papa insisted that they change their clothes before extracting milk from their breasts. This milk would be used to feed the babies in the incubators. After lunch and a long nap, the wet nurses would breastfeed the babies once again.

Papa believed that breastmilk was affected by fatigue, poor diet, worry, and lack of exercise. Papa wanted all the wet nurses to be healthy and happy so that his babies would grow and thrive. He believed the women should have no worries. If a problem was pressing on her mind, Papa encouraged Mama to talk to her. If money was her concern, Papa found a way to lend her money to reduce her stress so that she would produce the purest milk product.

I was never allowed to touch the babies, even when they were in their wicker cribs in the growing room. I viewed the babies in their glass incubators, just as the patrons did. After paying the admission fee, spectators paraded through the nursery, standing behind a barrier wall which separated them from the babies and the nurses. I hoped and prayed that I could hold a baby, but Papa was a trained physician who had strict rules for everyone, including me. I was not allowed into the nursery until I was older. You see, my father, Dr. Walther Baier, was a serious man when it came to the babies.